# THE LAND OF NOD 2: AND THE SEA GAVE UP THE DEAD

By

*ROBERT M WHITBEY*

ISBN: 978-0-578-85736-7

# PROLOGUE

The aging Cessna 172 buzzed through the air so slowly it barely maintained its altitude. Conner, the pilot, could hardly see the ground through the low clouds. He and his copilot and 16-year old daughter, Stephanie, squinted hard to make out familiar shapes on the ground.

"I think we're gonna have to decrease altitude, daddy," Stephanie advised.

"I think you're right, pumpkin," Conner replied. "Take us down to 5,000."

The girl pushed the handles forward slightly and the plane began to dip down through the clouds. The ground, at first, became much harder to see, then cleared suddenly as they broke through the cloud bank. There was still some slight ground fog to deal with, but the landscape and buildings were much easier to see now.

The city seemed to stretch on forever. Skyscrapers are not prevalent in Los Angeles. Most are scattered throughout the city. For Stephanie, they were no more than visible waypoints. She had never visited any of them nor did she remember even driving past. They were remains of a past world like Stonehenge or the Acropolis. That is, if those features had lights on them. And large groups of ravenous former humans.

"There's a hill coming up in about ten miles, but it crests at 2,500," Conner stated.

"Roger that," Stephanie acknowledged.

Stephanie glimpsed down through her side window. "Lots of movement down there."

"Yep. Ever since they stopped killing each other we're seeing more and more large groups."

"Should we buzz by Catalina again?" she asked.

"Nah, I don't see a reason to," her dad resigned. "No one there that needs to be saved. Just hundreds of zombies."

"I was really hoping it would be cleared out. At least, mostly clear," the girl lamented.

"Judging from all the wrecked boats, I bet a lot of people thought it would be safer there. It definitely isn't safe now." Conner shook his head as he made notes in the logbook.

"Fuel is near halfway. Should we head back?"

"Let's head a little further north," Conner instructed. "I want to take a look at Santa Barbara, then we'll tool over some of the islands out west before we head back out to the desert. Just bank over towards the coastline as usual."

"I wish the GPS was still working," Stephanie stated.

"I know it's easier, but you're using the old school instruments very well now, girl. Even at night."

Stephanie smiled without looking at him. Conner never had a problem complimenting his children, but he didn't do it lightly. She knew that if he said it, he meant it. "Are we near Oxnard?"

"Yeah," he responded almost absently. "Drop down to 3,500," he instructed with some concern in his voice. He leaned closer to the side window and stared down.

Stephanie pushed the handles forward again, dropping down until her instruments indicated 3,500 feet. "What is it daddy?" she asked peering out the side window. Far below them, the ground seemed to be alive with movement. "Is that…people?"

"Used to be," he replied with dread in his voice. "They're infected. Tens of thousands of them. All heading north along the PCH."

"I've never seen so many all in one place. It stretches on for miles. Looks like it tracks back all the way to Los Angeles. Maybe even Anaheim."

"They're following the contour of the land. Look out in the distance." He pointed to the right of the plane's nose. "That's Santa Barbara. It's not quite swamped yet. If they keep heading north, they may stay on the '1' or the '101' or both. That spans the whole length of California. Anyone within fifty miles of the coastline will be in the way of this…swarm."

"I hope there's no one living north of Santa Barbara," Stephanie noted. "If so, they need to move."

5

# CHAPTER 1

"Got you!" Nod yelled, pulling Lizzy to the ground as the two ran. They rolled as they hit, with Nod taking the brunt of the impact on his back. Lizzy giggled to the point of breathlessness as Nod held her. "Can't outrun the old man," he told her, with a quick peck on her temple.

"Not fair," she squeaked. "You're too fast!"

"That's right!" Nod yelled triumphantly as he released her. "No three-year old can beat me!" He raised both arms in the air with his back still on the ground.

Lizzy ran back to the large group of youngsters congregated on the other side of the yard where the elderly but spry Bob Floss was beginning a magic show. Nod stood and walked back to the porch where several adults were watching the yard.

"You could have let her win," Sadie Miller suggested, dusting his shoulder off.

"Hey, you tag me and yell 'you're it', you take your chances." Nod laughed. "Age matters not." He reached for the brown bottle he had been holding when Lizzy made her play. "How are we fixed for Dean's home brew?"

"We have plenty," Sadie replied. "My boy's been brewing like crazy ever since we found that supply of empty beer bottles last summer. Every flavor you can imagine." She glanced over at her son, Dean, who sat holding his six-month old daughter, Trinity, as he talked with a group of men. His wife, Millie, was pregnant with their second child, but still ran the kitchen today.

"Tell me about it. Have you tried the peanut butter cup IPA yet?"

"Ooooh, yeah. Have you had the peppermint dark brew?"

Nod made a gagging sound. "Thankfully, no. I thought I had seen every possible flavor combination when I lived in Portland. Dean's an evil genius."

"He prefers the title 'Sweet Barley Brainiac.' I think he made a t-shirt." The two shared a laugh.

Nod took a long pull from his bottle, emptying it. He looked at the unlabeled glass and remarked, "Humans, huh. Not even two years after the zombie apocalypse and were already blessed with craft beers."

"Like you always say," Sadie replied. "Priorities." She took his hand and squeezed it playfully.

Nod turned to look out at the large yard of the Miller Ranch and all the people it contained. Last year, at a party for Lizzy's second birthday, it was just a handful of people. Now, with the addition of several other local groups and even more 'refugees' from the south, there were over eighty people ranging in age from six-month old Trinity to mid-70's Bob Floss. Most were in their 20's and 30's, like Nod.

"So, what's the final count on the number of birthdays we're celebrating today?" Nod asked.

"Eight people have birthdays in March," Sadie replied. "A few of the younger kids didn't know their birthdates, so we picked some days for them like we did Lizzy." Sadie took a sip from her bottle. "How are the crops coming?"

"All of the gardens are good to go," Nod stated. "The field crops are mostly planted. We've got some big crews and lots of tractors so the work is fairly quick. Turns out some of the 'refugees' were involved in farming and that one new guy—Pete *something*—he has a degree in Crop Science."

"Sheesh, he's a score," Sadie remarked, then furrowed her brow. "I'm sorry. That sounded terrible."

Nod scoffed. "I know what you mean. And it is a big score for us. He's really smart about this stuff. He wants us to automate everything so we need fewer people to tend the crops. Since most of the vineyards were already rigged for it, it should be easy. Well, easier than starting from scratch, anyway."

"So, what happened with the satellite internet connection? Your team have any luck yet?" Sadie asked, scooting a little closer to Nod as they sat on the wooden porch.

Nod smiled. "Oh yeah. The communication satellites are still up there and still transmitting, according to Cindy

Testor. Man, she is a heck of a hacker. Did I tell you she studied Computer Science at Cal Poly?"

Sadie's smile faded almost imperceptivity. "I think you said something about that."

"After she got the radios set up, she was able to establish links with several satellites up there. It's not the full internet, but it's something. Still no communication with anyone, though."

"Is that why you haven't been on any runs with us in a while? Working on the techie stuff with Cindy?" There was a certain lilt to her voice when she pronounced 'Cindy' and Nod noticed it.

"Oh, no, no. It's not like that…" he stammered. "She's a friend and that's it." He took her hand into his.

"Hey, I get it. She's smart and pretty and young." Sadie's voice was playful but Nod corrected her anyway.

"And gay," Nod added.

Sadie's face relaxed. "What? She has a five-year old son."

"Yeah, from a brief fling in college," Nod stated. "You really didn't know?"

"Not a clue," Sadie said. "I guess I have no 'gaydar' anymore." Sadie thought for a second. "Is that why she's always with Sophia Abrams? Are they *together* together?"

"Yep. I mean, it's still early in their relationship, but I can see it lasting for some time."

"And why do you know all this?"

"People love to tell me things." Nod laughed. "And, frankly, I asked. Tech work is long and boring as you wait for this or that to boot up and initialize. We have to talk about something."

There was a silence as the two collected their thoughts for a few moments. Both scanned the area out of habit.

Nod finally broke the silence by whispering to Sadie, "Sophia says it's weird that her mom and girlfriend have the same name."

Sadie spat her beer out, trying to keep from laughing, which made both of them laugh harder. They huddled together like schoolchildren, laughing, and hoping no one would ask them why.

"I'm not kidding," Nod whispered through chortles. "She calls her Dee most of the time, now."

After a few more minutes of giggling and holding each other tight, Sadie asked, "Well, Nod, would you like to go for a walk around the property?"

"I'd love to," Nod replied.

Both got up and began to walk away from the people in the backyard. They held hands as they strolled along the tall chain link fence. Reaching the back gate, they both instinctively patted their hips where their ever-present sidearms were carried, then exited towards a conglomeration of large equipment, semi-trucks and trailers.

Sadie's oldest son, Dean, had been bringing in and parking anything he thought they might need at some point. Earth moving equipment, ATV's, military Humvees, et cetera. But Nod and Sadie both knew exactly where they were headed. They quickly moved through the equipment along a well-beaten path of weeds.

The large fifth-wheel travel trailer was situated near the pole barn at the far end of the property. It had belonged to the Miller family long before the viral outbreak that killed off most of the human population and turned others into rage monsters. The tires were flat and the paint was peeling off the metal, but inside was clean and quiet.

Sadie and Nod had been using this as their special 'getaway spot' for almost six-months. It wasn't that they wanted to keep their relationship a secret since everyone already knew about them already. It was more of a matter of necessity. The Miller house had Dean, his wife Millie and new baby as well as Sadie's teenaged son Tex. It was hard for them to be discreet with that many people in one place. So, Sadie had set up her old trailer to make things more convenient. She led the way as they entered, with Nod taking one last look around before following her inside.

\*\*\*

Forty-five minutes later, Nod and Sadie were returning to the party. They walked hand in hand, not rushing. The afternoon was turning to night and someone had turned on the strings of party lights outside. The lights ran along the top of the tall chain link fence that surrounded the large backyard and crisscrossed back and forth. There were so many tiny lights that no other outdoor lighting was necessary. Nod could see the adults standing around the inside edge of the fence and the kids playing in the middle. He smiled widely.

Sadie noticed his grin and quipped, "You're not gonna go run off and tell your buddies what we just did, are you?"

"What?" Nod responded. "Who... Why?"

Sadie slapped his shoulder playfully. "I saw your face just now. Your smile got really big, like you just realized something funny."

"Oh, no, well kinda." Nod's cheeks flushed a bit. "I was just looking at how normal everything is now. Well, normal for now, anyway. Look how everyone's just standing around, talking, while the kids play. Millions of Crazies all around us and it's like a block party in there. The only thing missing is the loud music."

"If there were loud music, all those Crazies would be coming here," Sadie replied. "And I know what you mean. I noticed a few people weren't even wearing pistols when they showed up. And there are fewer rifles propped against the porch than I can remember seeing since this all started."

"Probably because they know Dean has a bigger armory than anyone," Nod chuckled, unlatching the gate.

Once inside, Sadie turned and gave Nod a quick peck on the cheek. "I need to go see if Viv needs any help in the kitchen."

"Okay," Nod replied. "I'll mingle."

Nod scanned the yard and saw many of the groups were indeed mingling. The Millers, Abrams and Floss groups had been together since not long after the madness started. Though Nod lived with Viv and Lizzy a few miles up the road, he always considered them all part of the Miller's group. Though the groups were informally named after their patriarch's or matriarch's, all of them had absorbed other smaller groups of refugees looking to belong somewhere.

The newest group was usually referred to as the Hightower's after their leader, Dan Hightower. He and his son Dale were one of the first families to take in refugees. Their group had been based in San Miguel, a small town just a few miles north of Paso Robles. But after a fishing trip to Lake Nacimiento, just west of Paso Robles, Dan decided to move the group to the lake and live in a small resort there with lots of cabins along the lake. There was fresh water and fish and it was easier to defend, if needed. Nod and Dean had met them eight months ago when Dean wanted to find out if the lake had any good fish. The groups had been cooperating ever since.

Dan was the first person to notice Nod and motioned for him to come over. Nod waved and walked towards the group that included Dan, Dale, Tex and a few others Nod didn't know.

"Hey Nod, I haven't seen you in a while," Dan remarked.

"I was doing a perimeter check," Nod replied. He noticed Tex's eyes roll, but he had a smile on his face. "How is everyone doin'?"

"Still recovering from that barbeque," Dale stated, patting his belly.

"Sadie is a heck of a grill master," Nod agreed. "But I hope you saved room for some homemade ice cream. Should be ready soon."

"Lord help us all," Dale replied, shaking his head.

"How is that trench coming?" Nod asked.

"About halfway across, another five hundred feet or so," Dan answered. "Another two weeks, probably."

"If we don't stop work to clear more crop space," Dale added. "I really think we should have a bigger garden on site."

"You guys can do what you want," Nod responded. "But your people have been helping maintain our crops. As far as we're concerned, they are as much yours as they are ours."

"He knows that Nod," Dan stated. "He's just the type that likes to have a backup plan. His mom was the same way, God rest her soul." Dale smiled and put his hands in the air, signaling his 'guilt.'

"Nothing wrong with over preparing," Nod agreed. "I'll see if Pete can come over and help you pick out a good location, if you want. Dude knows a lot about soils and stuff."

"We would appreciate that," Dale responded.

"I still can't get over the idea that you are creating an island," Nod stated.

"Well," Dan mused, "It's more of a half island-half moat. The resort was on a peninsula already, we just need that trench dug to cut it off completely. Crazies can't do water."

"Well, I can't wait to see it," Nod said.

"Nod!" came the familiar shriek behind him.

He turned and answered. "Yes, Lizzy?"

"Dance?" she asked, her tiny hands clasped in front of her.

"You know loud noise brings the Crazies, Lizzy," Nod reminded her.

"But the lights," she argued.

"The lights are blocked by the trees and hills, Lizzy. We talked about this."

"Just a little dance?" she pleaded.

Nod relented, unable to deny his little girl. "Okay, but it can't be loud. Let me turn it on."

Nod walked over to the porch and found the small stereo attached to an old iPod. He pressed the 'play' button and slowly turned the knob until the music was loud enough to be heard around the yard, but not much further. The kids immediately began to dance around in the middle of the yard.

Nod walked back to the group he had been speaking with. "She loves bluegrass, for some reason." He laughed.

"Who doesn't?" Dale replied, taking the hand of his girlfriend, Maria, and trotting off to join the fun. Before long, quite a few adults had followed their lead.

Before long, Lizzy yelled toward Nod, "Come dance wiff me!"

Nod, who had always hated dancing, acquiesced, and began to move towards her. As he started to move his hips and shoulders to the music, he noticed something in the sky. He stopped moving and stared up. Others, noticing the odd behavior, followed his gaze.

17

"A satellite?" someone asked.

"I don't think so," Nod replied. He motioned to the porch and asked, "Can someone turn that down?"

As soon as the music stopped, every adult knew what they were looking at. Overhead, only a few thousand feet up, were blinking lights and the almost forgotten sound of propellers.

# CHAPTER 2

"What is that?" Lizzy asked.

Nod continued to stare at the lights as they continued north. "That's an airplane, Lizzy." He looked down at her. "Do you remember me talking about airplanes?"

"Like your drones?" she asked.

"Right, only bigger. Big enough to carry people," Nod stated.

"Or bombs," Dale added.

"Dale!" Maria chuffed, smacking his arm.

"Uh, right, sorry. It's probably people," he responded.

"It's headed north," Sadie stated, appearing suddenly next to Nod.

"It ain't military," Dean said. "I think it's just a Cessna or something like that."

"Sounds about right," Dan acknowledged. "Can't tell much from the lights, but the high pitch and slow movement screams Cessna. We used to see them all the time with the tourists wanting to tour vineyards from the air. I think they took off from Oceano instead of the bigger airport in San Luis."

"I'm willing to bet this one didn't come from either one of those," Nod added. "It's banking west towards the coast now."

They all watched until the flashing lights disappeared into the low coastal clouds. Slowly, people began to resume their discussions or start new ones about the sighting. Soon, Millie and Viv brought out the homemade ice cream and the festivities fully picked up again.

The party continued for another couple of hours, then groups began to leave. People were particularly good about cleaning up after themselves, so there wasn't much for the Miller's to do at the end of the night. Nod, Viv and Lizzy were the last to go.

As Nod drove, Viv sat in the passenger seat while Lizzy sat in the back in a large car seat. Viv yawned as she stared at the darkness outside.

"Tired?" Nod asked.

"I'm old, Nod. I'm always tired," she said with a chuckle. "I was just thinking about the lights."

"Wondering if it's a bad sign?" Nod inferred.

"I don't believe in signs, Nod. I just hope they're friendly. Or, at least, not bad people."

"Most of the people we've met are decent."

"Yeah, but not all of them. We've had our fair share of bullies and bandits the last year and a half. Obviously, the

Morton's were the worst, but our groups have had to deal with bad guys far too often for my blood."

"Way too often for a planet with so few humans left," Nod replied, thinking about the half dozen incidents Viv was speaking of. "But those were always half-crazed drifters. It takes some organization and competence to keep an airplane in working condition under the current circumstances."

Viv waved her hand. "I'm sure it won't turn into anything. Just an old lady musing on the what-ifs."

"You're thinking what everyone is thinking, Viv. Nothing wrong with preparing yourself mentally." Nod's voice showed no real concern, but inside his head, he was already sorting through the many possibilities those flashing lights in the sky could bring.

***

Two days later, Nod was working with a crew in one of the former vineyards, when Pete approached him.

"Morning, Nod," Pete said, his hand in the air. He was well-over six feet tall with thin hair and thick glasses.

"Hey, Pete. What's going on?" Nod replied.

"You know Pancho, right?" He pointed to his left, where an older man with long white hair stood. He smiled at Nod.

"Yeah, you're with Hightower, right?" Nod said with a slight head bow.

"Yeah, my granddaughter and me," he stated.

"Yeah, yeah, Maria's your granddaughter," Nod remembered. Pancho gave him a thumbs up.

"Oh good," Pete chirped. "I've been trying to get him over here for a while but he's been busy tending the Hightower's garden. He's a heck of a gardener!"

"Really?" Nod raised an eyebrow.

"Pancho and I go back, what, three years?" Pancho nodded his head. "When I worked in the county Ag office, I ran the Master Gardener program. Pancho was always at the meetings and knew WAY more about what grows around here than I did. I learned a lot from this guy." He smacked Pancho lightly on the shoulder and got a big smile in return.

"That's awesome!" Nod said excitedly.

"We're gonna do some recon because Pancho has some ideas about growing cactus. It's real exciting because we could use the cactus to ring the fields to protect us out here and use the cactus fruit and flesh for food. Very little water needed."

"That'd be great. Less people needed on security, more hands in the dirt," Nod stated.

"And *nopales* tastes soooo good," Pancho added with a smile.

"Oh, yeah," Nod responded. "I used to eat it on tacos. There was a hole in the wall place…" He trailed off as an odd sound began to fill the air. Heads were popping up all over the fields as recognition set in. It was the sound of an airplane again. And this time it was much louder.

"Which direction?" Nod shouted to no one in particular. They were surrounded by hills, so the sound bounced around.

"I think it's east," Pancho called out, pointing to the higher hill in that direction. "And the engine doesn't sound too good."

Nod didn't recognize the sputtering sound of the engine until Pancho pointed it out. Everyone in the field turned to the east as a bright yellow airplane crested the top of the hill. It rose slightly, then began to descend.

"It's a crop duster," Pete observed. "An old one."

"It looks to be heading towards the highway," Nod guessed. He looked around and saw Dean and several other guys running towards the trucks. Nod took off, too.

"No rifles, guys," Nod shouted. "Make sure you're wearing your pistols. We don't want to spook them."

Two trucks filled with people pulled out and onto the paved road. Highway 46, though in full view from where they were, was about two miles away. As fast as they were on foot, the trucks were still faster.

Pete drove the truck Nod was sitting in. "It's landing hard," Nod stated. The airplane's long front landing gear folded underneath the fuselage, sending sparks out in every direction. The craft twisted sideways as a wing tore off. The trucks arrived just as the buckled metal body came to a halt.

"Stop here!" Nod shouted when they were a couple of hundred feet away. "It might blow up."

As Nod got out of the truck, Dean blew by him running all out to get to the downed craft. Nod, and most of the others chased after. Smoke was billowing out of the front of the engine, but no flames were visible. Nod could see the pilot climbing out of the side window as he neared.

Dean hopped up on the remaining wing and put a hand on the pilots back to help. Nod could hear Dean's voice, but he wasn't yelling and the pilot was letting himself be helped. When Nod got there a few seconds later, the pilot was almost out.

"Careful, fellas, I think he's got a busted leg," Dean advised.

"Definitely busted," the pilot said through gritted teeth. "But I've had worse."

"Let's get him to Viv," Nod advised.

"She a doctor?" the pilot asked.

"Closest thing we got," Nod replied, putting one of the pilot's arms around his shoulder.

"That'll work," the pilot stated, a forced smile on his face.

Nod and Dean got him to a truck and with the other guys, placed him into the bed. Nod jumped into the back and they started the short drive to Viv's ranch. Nod could hear Dean on the radio advising Viv that they were on the way. Nod looked back and saw some people had stayed behind to make sure the fire didn't spread.

"As you can imagine, I've got some questions," Nod stated.

"Do you mind waiting a little while?" the pilot asked. "It's a little hard to focus right now and I'd rather tell the story to your whole group so I don't have to repeat it."

"How about a name?"

"Conner. Conner West," he replied. "And thanks for helping me out back there. The Air Tractor 400 is a beautiful plane, but she was over 30 years old and not really built for distance."

It only took a few minutes to get to Viv's ranch. The gate was already open and she was waiting by the door of her barn where the make-shift surgery center had been installed. As always, her two nurses-in-training, twin sisters Tina and Dina Floss, were there to assist her. They got him inside on the examination table, then Viv kicked everyone out.

"He said his name was Conner West and it was a good plane that wasn't meant to travel distances," Nod explained to Dean. "So, he's not from around here."

"I'm surprised he could tell you anything," Dean marveled. "The bone was sticking out of his leg." He shuddered.

"Well, thank God for Viv and a virus that makes us heal fast," Nod mused.

"If it doesn't kill you or turn you into a blood-crazed lunatic," Dean added sarcastically.

A few minutes later, Sadie arrived. They recounted the entire story to her as they sat outside and waited. An hour after that, Viv walked out and tossed her latex gloves into the burn barrel by the door.

"We got him sedated first so we could fix that leg," she explained. "Everything went back into place and he should be walking a few days. I'll x-ray it again tonight to make sure it's healing correctly."

"Did he say anything?" Nod asked.

"No, no. But he was rambling a bit after we sedated him. A lot of it was incoherent but he said the name 'Stephanie' several times. He did say something odd right before we put him to sleep, though."

She paused and massaged the back of her neck. Dean looked at Nod. Nod looked at Sadie. Sadie shrugged.

"And?" they all three asked in unison.

"He said, 'They're coming'."

# CHAPTER 3

"Who's coming?" Sadie asked.

"He didn't elaborate," Viv replied. "But his tone was dire."

"Great," Dean stated, sitting back down in his chair in an exasperated manner.

Sadie put her hand on her eldest son's shoulder. "Now, there's no reason to worry yet. We don't have any information."

"Except someone is coming and it scared this guy enough to fly away from them," Dean intoned. He picked his head up and looked at his mother. "Are we just gonna go from one fight to another? Survival is hard enough with the Crazies. I hate having to worry about what other people are gonna do, too. I wish we could just find an island in the middle of the ocean and move everything there."

"I'm with Sadie," Viv stated. "There's no need to worry yet. This guy, Conner you said, he's in good shape. Well-fed with trimmed beard and hair. Those coveralls were neat and tidy, other than what happened to them in the crash. Even his underwear was clean."

"You looked at his underwear?" Nod laughed.

"I'm old, Nod, not dead," Viv replied. "Besides, we had to cut those coveralls off of him. He's got a military tattoo on his shoulder. I think it's Army, but I can't be sure."

"When do you think we'll be able to talk to him?" Sadie asked.

"We'll make sure he stays out for a few more hours. That'll be long enough for his bones to begin to knit back together. I'd rather he not move too much until that happens. If he progresses like everyone else, he'll be walking day after tomorrow."

"I just want to talk with him," Nod said. "Can you let me know when he wakes and is lucid?"

"Sure, and I'll make a list of things I need replenished for the office."

"Awesome," Dean replied. "We're doing a run tomorrow and there are several clinics we haven't looked at."

"Let's get some lunch and radio out to the other groups what we know so far," Nod added. "Can we bring you guys anything, Viv?"

"Nah, me and the girls ate right before you arrived. You can feed Lizzy, though. She's playing in the back yard with the Testor boy."

"Oh, Schuler's here?" Nod asked. "Cool. Grilled cheese it is."

*** 

"It's like old times, huh?" Nod stated. "The three of us sitting together, scarfing down some lunch."

"Except we're not squeezed into a Humvee and scannin' for Crazies the whole time," Dean corrected. All three chuckled.

"Man, how many lunches did we have interrupted by a dozen Crazies appearing out of nowhere?" Sadie mused.

"And how many times did one of use almost get dragged away because they forgot how their rifle worked?" Dean remarked, giving Nod the side eye.

"At least five times I can think of," Nod said with a laugh. "It hasn't been that long, has it? Since we three went out on a run?"

"A few months, right?" Sadie remembered. "I haven't been out in a long time either."

"We've got lots of volunteers these days," Dean added. "I only go out once a week or so myself and usually just for specific things like Viv's medical supplies."

On the far side of the fenced yard, Nod saw Viv exit the door of her surgery room. She motioned for them to join her and the three adults stood up and began to walk over. As they passed the two children playing, Nod spoke to them.

"Now, you guys remember to stay in the fence. If you need anything, just yell. We'll be in Granny Viv's office."

Lizzy shrugged without taking her eyes off of her dolls while Schuler replied, "Okay, Uncle Nod."

Sadie's eyebrows raised. "*Uncle* Nod, is it?" she asked coyly.

Nod laughed uneasily and kept walking.

Inside Viv's office/operating room/recovery area, Conner was sitting up on the gurney. His broken leg was fixed straight out with an air cast holding it in place. He smiled as he spoke with his medical team but immediately turned to look at the three new people that had entered the room.

"You look better," Nod stated. He took the man's outstretched hand. "Conner, right?"

"That's right, Conner West," he replied. "And you said your name was... Nod?"

"Yeah," Nod replied without explaining. "And this is Sadie Miller and her oldest son, Dean. Dean's the one that pulled you out of the plane and drove us here."

Conner shook each of their hands, lingering a bit longer with Sadie than Dean. "I just can't thank you guys enough. I had that duster for almost twenty years and really thought she had twenty more in her."

Though Nod really wanted to clarify his 'They're Coming' statement, he thought he should ask some other questions first. "If you don't mind me asking, where are you coming from, Conner?"

"Pretty far," he replied. "My daughter and I have a small place outside of Palm Springs."

"Palm Springs?" Dean asked incredulously. "That's real desert, man. How have you survived out there?"

"Actually, we lucked into it. I knew there was a small airfield east of the city. When we got there, it turned out there was a huge solar field nearby. Plenty of water available for two people."

"And your daughter's name is Stephanie?" Viv asked. "You kept saying that name when you were zonked out on painkillers."

"That's right. Steph's all I got left."

"What about the Crazies?" Dean asked.

"Is that what you call them?" Conner chuckled. "We stuck with 'zombies' although we know they aren't dead. We haven't really seen many out in the desert. We didn't leave the airfield for months, then I ventured out to the small suburban area nearby. Found a lot of dead bodies and some dying zombies that were easy to finish off. I guess temperatures over 110 degrees are not conducive to their survival. Happily, we really haven't had much trouble from them or anybody."

"Let's cut the crap," Viv said bluntly. "Why are you here and what did you mean when you said, 'They're Coming'?"

Conner's face turned serious. "For the last year or so, my daughter and I have been doing recon flights over much of LA and the coast. We were looking for people that we might be able to rescue, at first. Then we started seeing the … Crazies building into larger and larger groups. Five days ago, we found that almost all of the groups coalesced into a single, gigantic Horde. I'd estimate over a million Crazies stretching out over most of LA."

"That's a scary thought," Nod expressed.

"I can assure you it's an even scarier sight," Conner assured him.

"But why come all the way up here?" Sadie asked.

"Because they are," Conner said with emphasis. "There's a million Crazies headed up the 101. Santa Barbara is already swarmed, but the line extends south almost to San Diego. My guess is they'll be as far as Pismo Beach within a week. Maybe earlier."

Everyone's face was semi-contorted as they sorted through what Conner had just told them. "I need a map," Nod suggested.

"I'll grab the one in the truck," Sadie stated and quickly ran out the door.

"Maybe we can destroy some bridges or something," Dean thought out loud.

"That's good thinkin', son, but I've scouted Santa Barbara over and over and I couldn't find a single bridge or choke point that would stop them. Maybe slow 'em down, but that's about it."

Sadie returned with the map and unfolded it. She then pinned it up on the bulletin board. "So, we are here." She put a red pin on the map. "And Santa Barbara is here." She put a green pin where she was pointing.

Dean walked over and began tracing the road between the two pins. "You're right, we'd need some serious ordinance to block their way."

"I've got some serious ordinance, son," Conner interrupted. "Ever heard of Marine Corps Air Ground Combat Center 29 Palms?"

"Yeah, out in the desert by 29 Palms," Dean replied with a hint of sarcasm.

"Exactly. It's just a few miles north of where I live. And it's fully stocked with every kind of boom machine you can imagine. I've been there and I can assure you it's easy to get to."

"You're kidding," Nod stated. "No vaults or bunkers or anything?"

"Nope, I think they were getting ready to deploy a lot of hardware 'when the balloon went up.' Ordinance and dried up bodies everywhere."

"Balloon?" Nod questioned.

"When the 'shit hits the fan,' Nod," Viv said.

"Did you notice any *big* bombs?" Dean asked.

"Oh yeah. Keep in mind, when I served, I flew Blackhawks for the most part. I never learned how to fly a jet or even a bomber, so my plan was to drop a 500-pound bomb from a Blackhawk. I just couldn't find a spot that would do any good."

"Shell Beach," Dean suggested.

"Where's that?" Nod asked. He searched his memory from before the virus but they were just visitors back then and had driven all around the coastal areas.

"Just south of Pismo," Dean explained. "The 101 snakes around the side of the mountain. I think it's six lanes, all attached to the mountainside. But there's no more than 100 meters between the side of the mountain and the ocean. If that part of 101 was gone, there's nowhere for them to go but back south."

"Conner?" Nod asked, looking to him.

"I didn't fly that far north," he shrugged. "I was hoping I could stop them at Santa Barbara. I'm not familiar with this area but if what you say is true, that might do it."

"I think I drove over there to get to Pismo," Nod remembered. "Before the outbreak, I mean. It sounds familiar."

"Hey, Conner," Sadie interrupted. "You said you have a daughter. Where is she?"

"I forgot about that," he replied with a raised eyebrow. "How long ago did I crash?"

"About five hours ago, give or take," Viv answered.

"Well then, she's most likely in a Lakota on her way here."

"Lakota?" Sadie asked.

"Small military chopper," Dean replied.

Conner winked and pointed at Dean. "She's got a lot of hours in it and it's pretty easy for one person to fly. And you don't need a runway to land. Our long distance radio communication has been spotty lately. I lost radio contact outside of Bakersfield. The plan was that if we lost contact, she should wait six hours, then follow my flight path and come looking."

"But it's only been five hours," Sadie stated.

"She's not very good at listening to me," Conner replied. "Gets that from her mother." He shifted to look at Dean. "If you could take a can of white paint or chalk or something out to the crash site and draw a large 'S' on the road and circle it, that's the signal that I'm okay and she should land. There was a can of spray paint in my duster, but I'm sure it's gone."

"No problem," Dean said. "I'll swing by my place and grab a couple of cans."

"I'll come with you," Nod told him. "Sadie?"

"I'll hang out here," she answered.

Nod smiled in reply, then followed Dean out the door. It took only a few minutes to drive over to his place and get the paint. Then a few minutes more to get back to the crash site. Neither spoke much as they drove, processing the information they had just received. Soon, they stood by the road, each one holding a can of spray paint.

"Is this a good place to land a helicopter?" Nod asked.

"No trees or poles nearby," Dean replied. "Road is raised up a little. Seems good." He began drawing the large 'S' on the road. A few people from the field had walked over and Nod began explaining what had happened. By the time he had finished, so had Dean.

"That's a good-lookin' circle," Nod pointed out.

"It'll do." Dean paused and looked up to the sky. "So, do we just wait?"

Nod dropped the tailgate of the truck and sat down. "I guess so," he resigned. He picked up the radio and let Sadie know what was going on.

Twenty minutes later, they heard the cutting sound of rotors. It wasn't the deep sound of a large helicopter, but it

36

was definitely audible from several miles out. Soon, the dark green helicopter was visible to their east and Nod and Dean, joined by the few remaining work crew members, were waving their hands in the air.

Nod couldn't see the pilot but could tell she, assuming it was a 'she', was hesitating a bit. Instead of coming right over the painted sign, she flew a couple of circles around the area first. Then she began to descend and landed, skids right in the middle of the circle.

The helicopter was bigger than Nod expected, considering Dean had called it 'small.' About the size of an air ambulance with room for six to seven people plus two pilots. The girl, who Nod estimated was in her mid-teens, stared at the small group intently as she unbuckled and took off her helmet. Wisely, Nod had asked three of the ladies that had been part of the field crew to stay and be part of the greeting party. It was those three that stepped forward to welcome her. The girl stepped out, a rifle slung in front of her, but her finger off the trigger.

One of the ladies, Nod thought he remembered her name was Sara, spoke to her first. "Your dad's gonna be fine, sweetie. He just broke his leg and our doctor is treating him." She held a radio. "Would you like to talk with him, first?"

The girl reached out cautiously and took the radio. She depressed the large button and spoke. "Daddy-o?"

A few seconds passed before the reply came. "Yeah, Pumpkin, I'm fine. I busted my leg and they are being very hospitable. There's two guys, Nod and Dean, who will bring you to me." Nod and Dean both put a hand up in unison.

"Alright, I'll see you soon, Daddy," she answered. She motioned to Dean and Nod. "Let's go."

Nod thanked the ladies for sticking around and pointed to the truck. "It's Stephanie, right?" The girl nodded and began to climb into the back.

"You can ride in the front," Nod advised.

"I'm good," she replied, keeping the rifle slung in front of her as she squatted down in the truck bed.

"Alright," Nod responded. He and Dean sat in the front seats and started back to Viv's.

"She's pleasant, huh?" Dean stated.

"She probably hasn't seen any other people in a year and a half. And she's worried about her dad."

"True. At least she has good trigger discipline."

A few minutes later, they pulled up to Viv's office. Nod opened the door and Stephanie peeked inside, then moved in when she saw her father sitting up in the gurney.

"What happened?" she asked, sitting her rifle in the corner and walking towards him.

"You can hug me first, girl," he instructed as he reached his arms out to her. Nod could see her body relax with the embrace. "I think it was the fuel. Plugged up the filter." His tone was tender but he spoke loud enough for those in the room to hear. She released him and pulled up a stool to sit nearby.

"We've started having issues with the AvGas," he explained. "That duster has had a full tank for over a year and the filter hadn't been changed in a long time. We've got a good supply at our airfield and another couple of large tanks at 29 Palms. All that time in the heat is starting to make the fuel chunky. We actually filter it through screens when we fuel up the Cessna or chopper. Takes forever, but it's cleaner and safer."

"Your Pop is gonna be fine," Viv reassured her. "I did a quick x-ray and the bones are already knitting together."

"Thank you, Doctor," Stephanie stated.

"You think I would be able to move in the morning, Doc?" Conner asked.

"I wouldn't recommend it," Viv advised.

"Doc, we have to do this tomorrow. The Horde is coming," Conner said.

"If you wait until mid-morning and use crutches, you should be okay. But you absolutely have to rest tonight. We know that eating and sleeping speeds the healing."

"We can do that," Conner answered excitedly. He turned to Nod and Dean. "Stephanie and I already had everything planned just in case we found a suitable target in Santa Barbara. She can take you through it tonight, then we'll fly out in the morning."

"All right," Nod agreed, looking at the other adults for support. Everyone seemed to agree.

"Do you mind if I have a few minutes with Steph before you leave?" Conner asked.

"Not at all," Sadie replied. "We'll wait outside."

# CHAPTER 4

"That was the best tri-tip I've had in years!" Stephanie stated emphatically. She sat back in her chair and noticed the others around the Miller's table had finished already.

"That's why we call mom the grill-master," Tex agreed.

Sadie blushed. "Have you guys been eating much meat?"

"Mostly canned hams and tuna," Stephanie lamented. "And both of us are terrible cooks. We did find a house about a year ago that still had a frozen turkey and five pounds of bacon in the freezer. That was a good week."

"It hadn't spoiled?" Sadie asked.

"No, the house had its own solar array and batteries. That's not uncommon out in the desert. They even left the AC on so it was nice and cool."

"Must be lonely out there with just your dad," Tex suggested.

"I can't lie, it's been tough at times," Stephanie offered. "After my mom and brother died, we hunkered down at our house in the Imperial Valley for a month. Then dad started going out and scrounging for food and stuff. Eventually he made it to the airport and found his crop duster. He spent several nights checking it out and gassing it up. The hardest part was when he flew out to Palm Springs to check out the airfield. He was gone all day and I hadn't been alone that long in months. Gosh, I don't think I've ever been that alone before."

"Did he teach you to fly after you moved?" Tex asked.

"Oh no, I've been flying for years. But up to that point, it was always with him. Dad always took me and Cliff, that was my brother, up when he could. I didn't solo until a year ago. I prefer helicopters, but I'm pretty good with small planes, too."

"I don't mean to pry, but did you lose them when it all started?" Sadie asked.

"Yeah," Stephanie replied with a sullen tone. "Mom and Cliff and me were at home. Mom wasn't feeling well and was sleeping in her room. Cliff heard something going on outside and looked out the window. One of our neighbors was screaming and running around. He started to go outside when mom started yelling. He told me to go to my room and I did. I hid under my bed, listening to mom scream. Cliff was holding her door shut so she couldn't get out. Eventually she broke through and I heard them wrestling around in the hall. Then mom came to my door and kicked her way in. Luckily, dad came home before she found me. He had to…put her down." There were tears in Stephanie's eyes and her hands gripped the chair arms as she spoke, but she didn't break down.

"I'm so sorry that happened to you," Millie, Dean's wife, told her with tears in the corners of her eyes. "We've heard a lot of similar stories. It's just terrible."

Stephanie forced a smile. "It's okay. It's probably healthy to share your story, right?"

"You're a strong young lady, you know that?" Sadie stated.

"Thank you, ma'am," she replied and looked around. "Maybe we should talk about the plan tomorrow?"

"Sure," Dean agreed.

"Before we do, can we talk a little bit about back-up plans?" Nod suggested. "It's just that these things never seem to work out exactly as planned. What should we do if we can't stop the Horde?"

"I suppose we could just get out of their way? Move somewhere for a while?" Sadie stated.

"Can't go north or south," Dean thought out loud. "West is the mountains and ocean. East is the Great Central Valley."

"You do not want to go to the Valley," Stephanie warned. "A dam up in the hills broke last winter. A lot of the valley is swamp now and really hot. And tons of zombies, sorry, Crazies. They're all over the place from the Grapevine north to Fresno. I'm surprised they haven't moved this way."

"Maybe head west, then. Towards Morro Bay," Dean posited.

"Highway 1 splits off of the 101 at San Luis," Sadie said. "This Horde will probably split and some will head that way since it's fairly flat. And the '1' goes right through Morro Bay then heads north along the coastline."

"And those mountains aren't very steep," Nod added. "We've seen them climb some pretty steep grades if they see something alive."

"Keep in mind that daddy says it may take months for them to pass through this area," Stephanie added. "If you want to hold up somewhere, you may have to stay there for two or three months."

"How about an airlift?" Nod stated. "Do you guys have access to anything large enough to move eighty people?"

Stephanie thought for a moment. "There are some passenger jets and cargo jets at 29 Palms. But they haven't been used in a long time and it'd take a lot of work to get them air-worthy. Plus, we'd need a good-enough landing strip for that large an aircraft. Plus, I don't think Daddy ever flew a jet."

"And we would need to move enough supplies for eighty people to last three months," Nod relented. "You're right, going to your place is out."

"It's too bad, though. Our airstrip is really close to a small subdivision. There would be plenty of room."

"We'd just have to drive a caravan of buses and trucks through tens of thousands of Crazies to get there," Dean acknowledged.

"True," Stephanie agreed.

***

They assembled at the helicopter the next morning. Nod, Dean, Millie, Sadie and Stephanie stood outside while Conner sat in one of the pilots seats running through the pre-flight checklist. Nod's group had brought backpacks with a few supplies and ammunition for their rifles and pistols.

"So, you'll just head out to the desert, get the bombs, refuel, drop the bombs and come back, right?" Sadie asked.

"Yep. If it all goes smoothly, we should be back by dinner," Nod assured her. She hugged him tightly then did the same to Dean.

"Okay, folks, it's time to go," Conner announced. Stephanie climbed into the other pilot's seat, while Nod and Dean climbed into the back. They buckled in and slid the doors closed. The helicopter rose into the sky slowly as Sadie and Millie backed away to the truck. Nod waved one last time as the two girls slowly faded from his field of view.

Once they were in the air and moving south east, Conner called them over the radio headsets. "It'll take us about an hour and a half to get there. I'd love to let you sightsee but we don't have the time or fuel." Both men gave him a 'thumbs up' showing they understood. "We'll land at

29 Palms. The Blackhawk we'll use to drop the bombs is ready to go. We serviced it and filled the tanks a couple of days ago."

Nod noticed Stephanie look out the side window suddenly and then back to her front. He didn't see anything, so he didn't ask her why. He thought her face looked uneasy for a second, but it was gone now.

Conner continued, "You guys will refuel this chopper and grab the bombs while I do the pre-flight on the Blackhawk. Steph will show you how to do everything." Again, they gave the thumbs up. In truth, Stephanie had been over the plan several times the night before, but it never hurt to go over it again.

Though most of their flight was over open land, Nod enjoyed what he could see. He never thought he would be in the air again and loved every minute. He did see that most of the city of Bakersfield was in ruins most likely from the water that had come down from that broken dam Stephanie had mentioned. Most of the houses in the area west of town where he had lived were barely sticking out of the standing water.

The base was much larger than Nod expected. Conner was almost certainly correct when he speculated that they must have been mobilizing when the outbreak hit. There were jets, tanks, helicopters and piles of ordinance everywhere. From the air, they looked like cheap plastic toys lined up by a six-year old right before he pelts them with rocks. But Conner didn't hesitate to bring them down.

Once the skids hit the blacktop, there was relief in Conner's face. "We only had about 10 minutes of fuel left. This one's not built for distance," he yelled over the sound of the rotors winding down.

"That was cutting it close, don't you think?" Dean yelled back.

"Like my barber always says, if you're gonna cut it, cut it close," Conner replied, rubbing his closely cropped hair. "Isn't that right, barber?" He nudged Stephanie as she took off her headset. She smiled back at him.

They quickly went to work. Stephanie showed Dean how to gas up the smaller helicopter, then had Nod follow her to what she called the 'bomb pile.' It turned out to be aptly named.

"They look like missiles," Nod remarked. "Stacked like Lincoln Logs."

"Dad says all bombs look like cigars," Stephanie stated. "Makes them more aerodynamic or something. There's a forklift over there made for moving these," Stephanie said, pointing to a large metal building. "I'll grab it unless you want to."

"I've never driven one, so knock yourself out," he replied.

She disappeared behind some Humvees, then returned a few minutes later with the forklift. Nod guided her towards the pile and secured one bomb to the forks.

Stephanie then motioned for him to follow as she led him to the Blackhawk.

Once they arrived, Stephanie guided the bomb into the cargo area. Nod helped move it into place then strapped it to the floor.

"Just two straps holding it in place, huh?" Nod observed.

"The straps are strong," Conner said from the pilot's seat. "They'll hold. We can fit three back there side by side."

They repeated the process two more times. Dean, who had finished fueling the smaller helicopter, helped with the third one.

"So, all we have to do is pull the pins out of the strap, one by one and nudge them out the side?" he asked.

"It's low-tech, I know," Stephanie stated. "But it'll work and it doesn't take a lot of effort."

"You've done this before?" Nod asked.

"We did a test run out in the desert after we first noticed the Horde," Conner quickly interrupted. "It'll work."

Stephanie nodded her agreement, but something about her eyes seemed off to Nod. He let it go figuring it was just nerves. She was crouched atop three 500-pound bombs, after all.

"What about the weight?" Dean pointed out. "You've got an extra 1,500 pounds now. What's that gonna do for fuel consumption?"

"The Blackhawk has an extra tank attached." Conner leaned out the door and pointed to the belly of the helicopter. "We can do nearly 1,000 miles with that even with the heavy cargo and one of you guys."

"Rock, paper, scissor for who gets to make the big boom?" Dean already had his fist in his palm.

"I wouldn't think of depriving you of the opportunity to cause that big of an explosion," Nod stated, his hands in the 'surrender' pose.

"Sweet! I found a few AT4's I want to bring along, too. You know, just in case we need a little more BOOM! They aren't heavy, so it shouldn't add much weight."

"What's an 84?" Nod asked.

"Not 84. A-T-4," Dean replied, saying the letters and numbers slowly. "It's an anti-tank RPG. I put five in a big duffle bag."

"It shouldn't be a problem, just stow the bag in the passenger side since you'll be in the back anyway," Conner instructed.

"You and I will follow in the Lakota," Stephanie told Nod. "With just the two of us, we should have plenty of fuel to follow them and drop you guys back at your place."

"Sounds good," Nod agreed.

***

Less than an hour later, both helicopters were in the sky over Los Angeles. The Blackhawk led the way with Conner piloting and Dean strapped into a jump seat in the cargo area. The smaller Lakota trailed behind with Stephanie piloting while Nod sat in the other pilot's seat.

"I thought you guys might want to see what was headed your way," Conner said over the headset.

"It just goes on forever," Nod responded, forgetting to key the microphone. Several thousand feet below, masses of bodies moved and swirled, covering every street and open area as far as the eyes could see.

Nod was surprised that, outside of the Crazies everywhere, the city looked mostly fine. There were a few burned out buildings and dead vegetation was evident everywhere, but most of the buildings looked pristine. He had expected the skyscrapers to be toppled and fires still raging, like in old disaster movies.

They continued northwest towards Santa Barbara. Nod couldn't tear his eyes away from the masses of Crazies. While, at first, they appeared to be marching together, it soon became apparent to Nod that they were all moving slowly in many directions, but the overall direction was the same. Groups would begin to move east but the next larger group moving north would bump them north. It didn't look like there was a common goal. It was more like a cattle drive.

"I don't think there is anything drawing them up the coast," Nod stated, again without keying his microphone.

Stephanie replied through the headset—"Make sure you key you mic."—and pointed to the button.

Nod smacked his forehead. "Sorry," he said, keying his mic this time. "I said it doesn't look like they are being drawn up the coast. I imagined they would all be moving in unison. Silly, I know, but this is very different. It's like a lot of them were moving that way and the rest are joining in because they can't go anywhere else."

"I was thinking that, too," Dean's voice echoed on the headset. "It's weird."

"Yeah, it is weird," Conner's voice agreed.

Again, Nod noticed Stephanie look uneasy. She was hiding something and Nod was going to question her as soon as they finished their mission.

"We're about ten minutes out," Conner announced. "Steph, start hanging back now."

"Roger that," she replied.

The Blackhawk began to pull away, but not too far. The plan was for the Lakota to hang out two miles south during the bombing. From there they could observe. If anything went wrong, they would be available for search and rescue.

Soon, the two choppers were in place. Nod remembered the area as soon as he saw it. Dean was right. The area between the mountain and the ocean wasn't more than a football field in width. And the ocean side was a sea cliff. If they destroyed the road, the rubble would likely prevent the mass of Crazies from moving any further North.

"There's a lot of wind here," Conner observed. "Should be good to go, though. Dean, are you ready?"

"Got my tether attached and ready to pull pin number one."

"We're in position. The road is directly below. On your mark."

"Pulling now," Dean replied. After a few seconds he stated, "Bomb is free but it's not moving out. Chopper is moving too much."

"Trying to keep her steady, but wind is buffeting us a little," Conner advised. Suddenly, the chopper dropped thirty feet, causing Dean to fall on his butt. The loose bomb had just started to roll out when the drop pulled it back inside. The collision with the middle bomb knocked the other two free and all three fell out one side. The shifting weight of the bombs turned the Blackhawk almost sideways causing it to descend very quickly. Dean slid toward the open door but was caught by the tether just inside the door.

"Brace yourself!" Conner yelled as he fought the controls.

The craft rolled back in the opposite direction, sending Dean towards the other door. His hand caught the edge of the jump seat before the tether extended out completely. He turned his head to see a ball of fire rolling up towards the Blackhawk.

Conner pulled hard on the stick, pulling the nose upward, throttling up at the same time. The fireball hit the tail section first, then moved up the side to the open doors. For half a second, only the nose was visible, then the entire helicopter rocketed upward.

Fire clung to the sides as the chopper spun back and forth with Conner fighting hard to regain control. Dean had a good grip on the jump seat but couldn't pull himself up into it. He could hear Conner's curses over the wail of the struggling engine.

"Daddy!" Stephanie yelled, easing the smaller chopper towards the Blackhawk.

"Stay back!" Conner screamed over the microphone. "Gimme room!"

Smoke was pouring from the tail rotor leaving a dark trail in the sky as the craft limped shakily towards the ocean then shifted towards the mountains. There were several high peaks nearby that rimmed the water's edge.

"We have to go after them!" Nod yelled to Stephanie.

"He needs room to right the craft!" she screamed back. "We'll be in the way!"

They watched together as the Blackhawk spun one way, then the other. It would gain altitude then lose it. It seemed like forever, though less than a minute had passed since Dean pulled the pin. As the helicopter summited a peak, the skids caught on several large trees. There was a small explosion, followed by a much larger one and the helicopter fell on the opposite side of the mountain.

"No!" Stephanie bellowed. She thrust the stick forward and after a few seconds they were directly over the peak. It was on fire and burning furiously. They descended slightly and moved away to get eyes on the Blackhawk. It was scattered down the side mountain. Fires burned in a trail behind the largest piece that had come to rest against a large rock. A body was visible sprawled on the ground halfway down the trail.

"No," Stephanie repeated softly.

Nod's eyes were wide and a lump was developing in his throat. Both of his friends were dead and for nothing. The three bombs hadn't even come close to destroying the road. The craft descended and Nod wiped his eyes, preparing to recover the remains of his friends.

"There's nowhere to land," Stephanie said weakly. "We'll have to come back for the bodies."

"I'm so sorry, Stephanie," Nod stated. He put his hand on her shoulder.

A series of small explosions went off in succession making Nod jump in his seat. This was followed by several hard impacts on the belly of their small chopper. Stephanie reacted by pulling up and away from the wreckage. Once she felt safe, she leveled off and hovered again.

"Did that do any damage?" Nod asked. He glanced around and outside the window.

"I don't think so," Stephanie replied, staring at the instrument panel. "Wait! We're losing fuel."

"Can we make it back?"

"We can try," she replied. She turned the nose and headed northeast towards Paso Robles.

Nod saw the landscape moving fast below them. They were just barely above the hills and Stephanie already had them moving faster than they had before. Several minutes passed by.

"We're not gonna make it," Stephanie advised. Warning lights and bells began going off.

"San Luis is right ahead," Nod stated and pointed forward. "The airport is on the east side. It's wide open."

"I hope it's not more than a couple of miles," Stephanie advised.

Nod felt the throttle dial back although Stephanie hadn't touched it. They were also descending but not too fast. The pitch of the engine was getting deeper. Luckily, the airport came into view.

"There! You see it?" Nod asked excitedly.

"Yeah, it's gonna be close," Stephanie spat between clenched teeth.

"You can do it, Steph!" Nod assured her.

The chopper flew a straight line towards the middle of the runway and Nod knew it was going to be a hard landing. When they were nearing the ground, the rotors miraculously sped up and slowed the descent. The skids bent when they hit but didn't break. Nod let out a breath he hadn't known he was holding.

# CHAPTER 5

"We gotta go!" Nod yelled, tapping Stephanie on her shoulder hard enough to snap her out of her focus.

"What?" she asked, as if just realizing he was there.

"Crazies," Nod explained. He was already unstrapped and opening his door. "San Luis is filled with 'em. And they had to have spotted us coming down."

Stephanie began to unbuckle herself and by the time she had gotten out, Nod had already grabbed their things from the back. He took her hand and led her away at a quick walk. He picked up his pace when he heard a feral screech in the distance.

"Head for that small building," he said softly.

Their destination appeared to be some sort of garage. It wasn't big enough to house an aircraft, but there were aircraft parts in front of it and it looked to be made of steel. They ran through the open door and Nod closed it gently behind them.

Inside was dark, but there was some light from two large windows in the ceiling. Other than some heavy equipment, it appeared empty. Nod saw a heavy piece of equipment by the door and began sliding it in front.

"Let me help you," Stephanie offered.

Working together, it moved a lot easier. Nod handed her the rifle and her backpack.

"Spread out and check for any other openings," he ordered. "Remember, don't fire unless you absolutely have to."

Stephanie gave him a thumbs up and slowly moved along the right side wall.

Nod pulled his pistol. He inched forward along the left wall, scanning the ground for anything that might make noise. They had determined long ago that the Crazies had an incredible sense of hearing. After a few minutes, they met at the back wall.

"Side door was welded shut," Stephanie whispered.

"Guy probably got tired of his tools getting stolen," Nod replied softly. "Windows are painted over and ten feet off the ground. There's a grease pit in the middle of the floor. We should probably move there." Stephanie nodded.

The grease pit was no more than three feet wide and a little over 5 feet deep. It's ten foot length was covered by short railroad ties sitting side by side to prevent anyone falling in. When in place, the wood was flush with the concrete. And were thick enough to drive over. Three of the railroad ties were missing on one end.

Nod used his flashlight to scan the inside of the pit. It was less dirty than he expected and had a narrow set of steps to get in and out. He motioned for Stephanie to enter, then he followed.

Stephanie could stand upright, just barely, while Nod had to hunch over. There was enough light coming in through the cracks between the wood that Nod shut off his flashlight. There were a couple of step stools they used as chairs.

"Listen, Stephanie, I know you're hurting right now," Nod said softly. "I am, too, trust me, but we need to focus on getting back to safety, okay?"

"I'm with you, Nod," Stephanie replied, fighting her tears. "Just tell me what you need me to do."

"San Luis had fifty or sixty thousand people when the virus hit. I don't know how much you know about the virus, but about 30% or so became the Crazies. Maybe half of them died from exposure, probably less in our mild climate. That means San Luis has ten to fifteen thousand Crazies running around."

"I never knew it was so bad," Stephanie said. "There wasn't any internet out in the desert by the time we got there. We knew it was bad, but not that bad."

"That's why we've stayed away from highly populated areas. We mostly concentrated on Paso Robles and the surrounding area where the populations were lower. But we've come into town here a few times. Once to rescue a small group and another time to do some recon. We left a few supplies and maybe a way out."

59

"Is it far?"

"No, maybe a mile east. There's a large white shed at the edge of a ranch. There's some food and water bottles and a few guns. There's also a couple of electric motorcycles hooked to a solar charger."

"Electric motorcycles?" Stephanie asked skeptically.

"I know," Nod responded. "Sounds weird, but we found a bunch of them on a flatbed a year ago. I guess someone up in Santa Cruz makes them. Made them. We kept all but the two we stashed here."

"Why electric?"

"They don't make any noise. Like none at all. We can follow the train tracks through town, then there is a trail that runs north into the hills. The Abrams ranch is about twenty miles further up."

"Train tracks? Shouldn't we just stick to the outskirts?"

"We haven't explored those areas so I don't know what we'd find. There's a road along the tracks and it's mostly fenced on each side."

"What about a radio?"

"I have a handheld in my backpack, but we're too far from our network of repeaters. The bikes are our best bet."

"How long do we have to wait?" Stephanie asked.

"At least until morning," Nod explained. "They'll be roaming around here for hours and they have the advantage at night."

They spent most of the afternoon and evening in the pit, leaving only to relieve themselves. They ate some of the food Nod had in his backpack and napped on and off. Nod could tell Stephanie was crying a few times but didn't react outwardly since she was obviously trying to hide it.

He teared up several times himself. How would he tell Sadie about her son? And what about Millie, with a baby and pregnant? The normalcy they had carved out of the Apocalypse would never return. It should have been him in the Blackhawk.

After Nod returned from using the restroom, Stephanie cleared her throat lightly. "Did I wake you?" he asked.

"No, I'm not really sleeping, you know? I need to tell you something."

"Okay, shoot."

"Remember when I told you we had tried the technique for dumping the bombs once before?"

"Actually, it was your dad, but yeah, I remember."

"That wasn't completely true. We had tried it before, but it wasn't in the desert or anything. We dropped them on the Horde."

"Really?" Nod asked.

"Yeah. The bombs fell like they were supposed to but didn't really make a dent, you know? Dad was so excited to try and then kinda crushed when he realized it would take a lot more bombs and fuel than we had to really make a difference. It was embarrassing to him. That's why he said we tried it in the desert."

"It's not a big deal, Stephanie, but thanks for telling me."

"I'm just really bad at lying. It hurts me physically to do it. That's probably why I couldn't sleep."

"Yeah, I get it," Nod replied. "You know, I had a daughter once. She was younger than you but a good story always put her to sleep."

"I'm a little old for stories," Stephanie whispered.

"Okay, how about something informative? Like I said, I had a daughter and a wife that both passed when the virus hit. As I was about to join them, by my own hand, two bunnies came out of nowhere. A mommy bunny and a daughter bunny. At least, I assume that's what they were. My daughter loved bunnies. So, I didn't go through with it."

"So, seeing the rabbits made you less suicidal?" she asked with a yawn.

"Sounds silly when you put it that way, but, yeah, a little less suicidal. But every so often I see those bunnies again, often when I need it the most. And then, of course, when I died—"

"You died?"

"Just a little. Dean saved me. But while I was dead, I talked with my wife and she told me to move on. It was good closure." Nod smiled though his eyes were welled up.

"Why are you telling me this, Nod?" The weariness was more evident in her voice.

"Mostly, to make you tired. Also, to make you understand that death isn't the end. Something comes after and it's a kinda peace not possible on this planet."

Stephanie moaned a little in reply and Nod could tell she had drifted off. He didn't know if he helped her at all, but he knew he had tried. She could chalk the whole experience up to the fractured mind of a grieving man and Nod wouldn't blame her. But the story lifted his own spirits and soon he was drifting off, too.

They left the garage just before sunrise when there was just enough light to see where they were walking. The airport was situated at the edge of town, so most of the route was completely open. They didn't speak as they walked. Stephanie simply followed Nod, the rifle in her hands while Nod carried his pistol.

They arrived at the white shed just as the sun peaked over the hills. Stephanie saw two large solar panels sitting on the roof. Nod opened the door and they both stepped inside.

There wasn't a lot of space with the two motorcycles and a workbench full of supplies. Stephanie hopped up on the bench and drank from a new water bottle as Nod checked out the motorcycles.

"Damn!" Nod whispered sharply.

"What is it?" Stephanie asked.

"The battery's dead on this one."

"Was it hooked up to the charger?"

"Yeah, it was. I think the battery is just bad. Shoot!"

"Can we ride double on the other one?"

"Yeah, but it's not really made for that. The seat isn't very big and the battery won't last as long. But it should be okay."

"Probably better anyway. I've never ridden a motorcycle. Heck, I haven't ridden a bike since I was, like, five."

Nod gave her a questioning look. "You fly airplanes and helicopters and haven't ridden a motorcycle?"

"I've only driven a car once." Stephanie shrugged. "We mostly use an electric golf cart back home."

They packed a few water bottles into their backpacks and rolled the motorcycle outside. Nod slung his pack over the handlebars and made sure it was secure. Stephanie tightened the straps on her pack, then slung the rifle over it. Nod handed her his pistol to use if necessary.

"It has a silencer?" she asked.

"A suppressor," Nod corrected her. "And despite what you might have seen in movies, they aren't silent, just quieter. Use it only if something gets too close. You've got ten shots so make 'em count."

"Only ten?"

"California had some pretty strict gun laws before the virus. Truth be told, I hated guns back then. I didn't think any civilian needed to be armed. This one belonged to a friend of mine. A trucker named Al."

Nod climbed on the motorcycle and Stephanie followed, sitting behind him on the edge of the seat. She gripped him tight across his stomach and the bike pulled forward. The only sound was a slight hum from the engine and the gravel under the tires.

They rode back towards town. By the time they reached the railroad tracks, the sun was completely over the hilltop. Nod watched the dirt road while Stephanie scanned the sides back and forth. She saw movement every so often, but nothing came at them. Nod was right, most of the route was enclosed with fences on each side other than the crossings.

After a few miles, Nod motioned that they were turning right towards a residential area. Stephanie patted his shoulder signaling she understood. The motorcycle was even quieter on the paved roads. There were a few cars parked haphazardly in the road, but they didn't block their way.

Nod felt a chill suddenly. The cars didn't block their way, but they did slow them down and move them into a particular direction. This was a classic ambush scenario, one that they had encountered in Atascadero a few months back.

Instead of passing through the maze of cars, Nod quickly slowed and made a right turn across a few dying lawns and back to the east. Stephanie patted his shoulder and he looked in the rearview mirror. A dozen or so Crazies had come out of nowhere and were chasing them.

Nod throttled up and pulled away from. He prayed it wasn't a cul-de-sac he was driving on. He noticed a left turn ahead and hoped it would double back to the original road. They turned left followed by another left. As they sped back west, Nod saw the sign indicating it was 'Not a Thru Street' and his heart sank.

There wasn't enough time to turn around and go back up the road, the Crazies were rounding the corner already. Then something colorful caught his eye. As his vision focused, he saw two Easter decorations in the shape of rabbits. There was a large one and a smaller one. Nod smiled and pointed them out to Stephanie.

There was a carport that was open to the back yard. If the back yard was open to the street, as many of these houses were, Nod hoped they could drive right through.

Nod slowed the motorcycle as they neared. He heard three quick concussive explosions, the sound his pistol made when fired. He didn't take the time to look back, instead focusing on navigating through the open carport. To his great relief, the backyard was indeed open to the road they had been on originally.

He gunned the throttle through the back yard, sending up a stream of dirt and small rocks. The front tire hit a large piece of concrete edging that had already been pushed over and they sailed over the sidewalk and back into the street. Nod gunned it again and they flew up the street, away from the chasing Crazies.

Nod chose that street because it ended at a well-worn walking trail that took them over the hill and through the moderately forested area. After forty-five minutes of rough riding on a dirt tail, they were back on solid pavement.

Nod decided to take a break from riding. Despite the virus putting them all into better shape, the constant bumping around on the trail had done a number on his back. He found a shady spot and pulled over.

"I was hoping you'd pull over soon," Stephanie stated as she pulled her helmet off. "I really have to pee." She handed him his pistol and hurried towards a small clump of shrubs.

Nod put his pistol in its holster and did the same. When he finished, he returned to the bike and waited for

Stephanie. She emerged a few minutes later, stretching as she walked.

"Did you hit anything when you fired?" Nod asked, reloading his pistol.

"I think I got one of them," she replied. "But the others slowed a little."

"Man, these things are getting smarter," Nod remarked. "There was a time you could tear into them with a 'fifty-cal' and they wouldn't flinch. Now, they're building traps and ducking bullets."

"That was a trap?"

"Yeah, we ran into something similar a while back. The cars are arranged to make you slow down and go right towards them. Works on wildlife, too."

"Sheesh, that complicates things." Stephanie paused for a second, then asked, "How did you know you could pass through that house to get back to the main road?"

"Lucky guess," Nod replied.

"Really? 'Cause it seemed like you were pretty confident."

"Okay, it's silly but did you see the Easter decorations? The two bunnies?"

"Yeah?"

"Like I said, when I need help the most."

"That really is beautiful," Stephanie said with a tear in one eye. She wiped it away. "So that little girl of yours, Lizzy? She wasn't yours before?"

"Well, I'm not black, so..."

"You know what I mean."

Nod chuckled. "No, we found each other in the early days."

Stephanie snapped her fingers. "She was carrying around an old blanket with bunnies on it."

Nod smiled. "It's all I have left of them. And a few pictures from our cell phones."

Stephanie's face softened. "I don't have anything from my family. What few mementos we had are back at the airstrip. There's no way I could get back to it." She thought for a moment, then remembered, "The locket! My dad wore a locket my mom gave him years ago. He said I could have it when I got older. It was his good luck charm."

"First off, you can stay at Viv's place as long as you like," Nod assured her. "But we do have several small airstrips nearby that have aircraft there. We'd have to, you know, do whatever maintenance you guys do, but I don't see why they couldn't fly eventually. Of course, we have to deal with the Horde first."

"I think your best bet is the ocean."

"A tough one for eighty people. We'd need a cruise ship."

"Or a bunch of smaller boats that stay close together."

That made Nod think. There could be a lot of boats anchored at Morro Bay. They hadn't been there since the virus attacked but he and his family had seen it just before. There were dozens of boats nearby at that time.

"Well, either way we'll need to discuss it with the group," Nod conceded. "All of us have a say in this community."

"Us? You already adopted me, didn't you?" Stephanie stated playfully.

Nod smiled and was about to reply when a sound perked up both their ears. It was the sound of an engine in the distance and it was getting closer. There were enough hills and trees that Nod couldn't tell which direction it was coming from and they both scanned the area.

Soon, a Humvee came around a bend slowly and headed straight for them. As it pulled alongside them, Nod saw the smiling face of Tom Abrams.

"Well, that didn't take long at all," Tom stated as he opened the driver-side door. Nod noticed Ray Testor, older brother of his friend Cindy, getting out of the passenger side.

"You're a sight for sore eyes," Nod joked, shaking Tom's outstretched hand.

"Sadie's got everyone out looking for you guys," Tom started. "When you never showed up yesterday, we decided to wait until first light and come out. I thought you might take the old 'High School Lookout' trail like we did the last time we were here." He looked at Stephanie and stuck his hand out. "I'm sorry, we didn't meet yet. I'm Tom and this is Ray."

"Stephanie," she replied, taking the outstretched hand.

"Where's Dean?" Tom asked.

"Dean and Conner, Stephanie's dad, didn't make it," Nod said solemnly. "There was an accident and the bombs didn't get dropped in the right place. The Horde is still on its way."

"Oh my gosh," Tom whispered. He put his hand on his forehead.

"I'm sorry, Tom," Nod stated. He put his hand on his shoulder. "I know you've been friends since you were kids."

"Poor Millie," Ray said sheepishly. "Can we recover, you know, the bodies?"

"No," Stephanie chimed in. "The terrain is too steep, and the Crazies are probably all over it by now."

Nod was surprised by Stephanie's words. He thought she intended to do the recovery at all costs when they flew away. Perhaps she had time to fully process it, another kid forced to grow too fast.

"Did you radio in that you'd found us yet?" Nod asked Tom.

"No, not yet. Signal doesn't travel out of this little valley very well." Tom's words were shaky at first, but he recovered.

"Good, I don't want Sadie finding out this way. Can you give us a ride to the Miller's place?"

"Yeah, we'll load the motorcycle in the back," Tom stated. "You know, Tex is over at our place right now. Maybe we should tell him first, then we can make sure he's with Sadie and Millie when you tell them."

"That's a good idea," Nod replied. Then he immediately thought, "There are no good ideas."

# CHAPTER 6

Tex took the news as well as could be expected. He was obviously distraught and tried to hold back as best he could. But Cindy Abrams, the matriarch of the Abrams group, grabbed him up tight and the tears flowed heavily from them both. After a few moments, he pulled away with a forced smile.

"We need to go tell mom and Millie before word gets to them," he stated.

"Alright, Tex," Tom assured him. "Well go right now."

"You guys go ahead," Abel Abrams, the oldest sibling and former deputy Sheriff, told them. I'll bring Nod and my mom along in the other Humvee."

Tom waved in reply. Nod looked at Abel, wondering why he wanted to bring him.

"We need to hurry," Nod said. "I need to be there."

"We can talk on the way," Abel replied. The three of them hurried out to another Humvee.

As they pulled onto the road, Tom, Stephanie and Tex not far ahead of them, Abel started, "I know this is a bad time, but what are we going to do now?"

"About the Horde?" Nod replied. "I have no idea. We didn't have a backup plan."

"Did you see it?" Cindy asked.

"Yeah, it's just like they described. Hundreds of thousands of them."

"And the Great Central Valley?" Cindy checked.

"Also like they said. Full of water and Crazies."

"So, there's no way we can fight and no where we can run," Abel admitted, shaking his head.

"How about Morro Bay?" Nod suggested.

"We dismissed that already, didn't we?" Cindy reminded him.

"I mean, we get some boats from Morro Bay and head out to the ocean until they pass," Nod explained.

"We'd have to leave the bay," Abel suggested, rubbing his chin. "If they see or hear anything, they won't move on."

"Well, there's usually a lot of boats moored there," Cindy added.

They rode in silence as each thought deeply. When they pulled up, Nod turned to them.

"When you get a chance, you need to contact the other groups. Tell them it's got to be the water unless they have a better suggestion. We need a plan ASAP. We'll start seeing more Crazies in three days, most likely." Both nodded in understanding.

"Can I ask you a question, Nod?" Abel asked.

"Sure."

"What gave you the idea to use the boats? You didn't mention it before."

"It wasn't my idea. It was my newest daughter's." Nod smiled weakly and both Abel and Cindy returned it.

Nod opened the door and stepped out. Sadie was already sitting on the porch. She stood and smiled when she saw him. He saw her scan the cars for Dean, finally settling her eyes on Tex. Then she slumped down to her knees and buried her face in her hands.

***

Viv had to give Millie a sedative so she would calm down. It wasn't a great thing to do for the baby, but Viv was more afraid of the stress she was under. By the time the sun went down, Viv had taken Lizzy home while Millie rested comfortably in her bed with her daughter, Trinity.

While Sadie had been inconsolable at first, the realization that Stephanie had lost her father, too, seemed to snap her back to 'mom' mode. They sat together on the porch swing. Nod and Tex sat side by side with their feet hanging off the side of the porch.

"I remember when we lost dad," Tex stated, his voice low. "Dean wouldn't leave me alone for a month. Always there. I couldn't even piss by myself." They all chuckled.

"I remember how mad he was after the fight with the Morton's," Nod remembered. "He didn't talk to me for a week. When I finally cornered him, he said he was only mad because I used grenades without him." Again, lots of chuckles.

"How about you, honey?" Sadie asked, looking at Stephanie. "What's a funny thing you remember about your dad?"

She smiled. "He was always trying to protect me," she began. "Whenever we would go to a house, obviously he would go in first but there was never any zom—sorry, Crazies after the first few months. It was just too hot and dry in the summer. If we came to a house that had kids toys in the front, he would say 'I already checked this one' when I knew full-well he hadn't. He just didn't want me to see any dead kids. With all the death and destruction we had seen, he didn't want me to see that again."

"Sounds like a good dad to me," Tex chimed in. Grunts of agreement came from all assembled.

"Well Nod, what's our Plan B?" Sadie asked. "What are we going to do about the Horde?"

"I talked with the Abel about it earlier and they're gonna speak to the other groups," Nod recalled. "I think our best chance is to head for the ocean."

"Really?" Sadie remarked. "Can we do that?"

"In theory, yeah. Of course, we have to see what boats are available at Morro Bay. That's the closest harbor, right?"

"Yeah," Tex agreed. "But we don't know anything about boats. I can't even swim."

"Hopefully, we've got some experience among the groups," Nod lamented. "I don't know much either, but it's really all we got. Every other direction is worse."

"Then what do we need to do?" Sadie asked, beginning to stand.

Nod motioned for her to stay seated. "Tonight, nothing. Tonight, we're just gonna sit together, drink some terrible home brew and eventually try to get some sleep. Tomorrow can wait for the sunrise."

\*\*\*

By nine a.m. the next morning, a meeting had been put together. At ten a.m., Nod, Stephanie and Sadie were sitting in the backyard of Bob Floss. Several representatives from all groups were there and everyone else was available by radio.

Bob Floss, the oldest member of the community and patriarch of the Floss group spoke first. "I wanna start by saying how sorry we all are about Dean and Conner. They were both good men and we grieve with you folks." He tipped his head toward Sadie and Stephanie, who sat next to each other.

"Thanks, Bob," Nod replied for the ladies.

"Well, we all know what's headed this way, but can you tell us anything we don't know, Nod?" Bob inquired.

Nod stood to speak. "The bombs missed their mark but destroyed a large swath of Shell Beach. The 101 was fully intact, though. The Blackhawk crash started a few fires, but according to a report from the Abrams group, they burned themselves out." He motioned to Stephanie. "We saw large numbers of Crazies already at Santa Maria. Think hundreds, not thousands. You might call this the leading edge of the Horde but the numbers increased in density all the back to Santa Barbara. That's just over a hundred miles with a lot of steep climbs. They won't be here for four days or so. But the leading edge will be here in two to three days."

A collective gasp went out between the group. There was a lot of whispering back and forth and some were definitely animated. Nod sat back down while Bob stood up.

"Now, folks, we knew this was coming. We know we can't head to the Great Central Valley because it's almost as bad there. We can't head north because that's the direction they're headed. Obviously south is out of the question. So that leaves west, to the ocean."

"Can't we just hunker down?" The younger Hightower, Dale, asked. "I know at our place, we've finished the cut away so we're essentially an island now. Plus, we're up in the hills, miles from the 101. They may just pass us by."

"They might," Stephanie chimed in. "But we've been watching this Horde for a while. The main body moves in one direction, but the edges go off and return. It's almost like a cloud."

"Or lava rolling down a hill," Nod added. "The overall movement is forward, but the sides follow the path of least resistance. If enough bleed off in one direction, a lot of the others will follow. And it's long enough that it may take months to pass."

"Still," Dale countered. "The ocean just seems so extreme. And no one in our group has much experience on open ocean other than some fishing trips."

"I'm a former Navy man, myself," Bob Floss revealed. "But this is something else. It'll be a huge, coordinated effort to make this happen safely."

"A few of our people spent time on boats and one was in the Coast Guard a long time ago," Abel stated. "They agree that it'll be hard, but it's do-able if there are enough boats."

Dale Hightower stood and spoke. "We took a vote last night and our group is gonna stick it out. Anyone that wants to stay with us is welcome to. We've got supplies for a year at this point. So, any plans you make, you've got twenty less people to worry about."

"I think we can all appreciate where you're coming from, Dale," Bob assured him. "And we'll let you know if anyone wants to join up. And same goes for your folks, we have room if they want to come along."

"Thanks," Dale replied and sat back down.

Cindy Abrams, who had remained silent up to this point, stood with a pad and paper in her hand. "Then it comes down to this. We need boats, food and water for sixty people. We need warm clothes and a way to clean them. Those boats need bed space for sixty. Hopefully, they all have bathrooms. We'll need toiletries for sixty including feminine products."

"I'll go to Morro Bay today and scope out the boat situation," Nod offered. "I'll need some folks with boat experience and some shooters. We haven't been there to scavenge yet."

"We'll take two Humvees," Abel suggested. "Sophia and the three others can come with me. Tom can drive another with you and some of the Floss group."

"I'll ask for a few volunteers," Bob responded. Behind him, several young men, including his grandson Clint, raised their hands.

"Why don't we get going and the other can handle the rest of the list?" Abel asked.

"That's a good idea," his mother, Cindy, replied. "Take some gear in case you need to stay overnight."

Most of the Abrams group departed to get their gear while Nod waited with the others. He had brought his supplies just in case and didn't need to go back home for anything. He listened as they divided the list of chores and made plans for some supply runs over the next two days. Soon, the meeting was breaking up and the two Abrams Humvees were pulling back in.

Abel drove the lead Humvee, with his sister Sophia in the passenger seat. Nod faintly recognized the other three sitting in the Humvee but Tom explained who they were on the way. Two of them were mid-thirties twins, Steve and Samantha, who had grown up wealthy and spent a lot of time on their grandfather's yacht. The other passenger was Cal, a mid-forties accountant that spent time as a young man in the Coast Guard. In a stroke of luck, he had been stationed for a time at Morro Bay.

Tom's Humvee had Nod in the passenger seat. Behind him were Clint Floss, who was the same age as Tom. They didn't know each other before the virus, but they were good friends now. Tina Floss, Clint's younger cousin and a nurse working with Viv had asked to come in case anyone needed medical attention. Rounding out the group was Wendy, a mid-twenties woman Nod knew nothing about except that she was usually very quiet.

From their current location east of Paso Robles, they could take Hwy 41 straight through to Morro Bay. Pre-virus, the drive would take about an hour. Now, Abel estimated two to three hours. The road would take them through

Atascadero, where lots of Crazies resided. Beyond that, Hwy 41 became a curvy, single lane road that could be full of cars.

As they entered Atascadero, they came across many spots where prior battles had taken place. The gas station on the corner. The school cafeteria up the road. The doctor's office one street over. Shell casings and decayed bodies littered these areas. Each of the groups had spent time making supply runs to this town and they had cleared out many of the Crazies as they did. Halfway through town, they hadn't encountered any of them.

"Seems pretty dead, if you'll pardon the pun," Clint remarked from the '.50 Cal' perched on top. "Probably not that many left anymore."

"It's all ambushers, now," Nod replied. "The smarter ones are all that's left."

"Kinda like us, right Nod?" Tom added.

"Speak for yourself. Some of us are just lucky," Nod laughed.

Nod saw some movement and immediately grabbed the radio microphone. "On the right, coming down the freeway ramp. We got a roller."

"Copy that," came Sophia's voice.

Their Humvee sped up as did the one Nod rode in. They passed the freeway ramp just as the abandoned SUV rolled past behind. It smashed into two parked cars.

"Man, I can't believe they figured out how to roll cars at us," Tom stated.

"Never gets boring," Nod replied.

Soon they were out of the small town and into the curvy single lane highway. Both Humvees had switched gunners, so there would be fresh eyes outside. The lead Humvee did have to push their way through a few wrecks, but the burned-out metal was fairly easy to move. As Nod had expected, they didn't encounter any Crazies on this leg of the journey because "Crazies hate open areas."

The view began to open up and the air outside was getting cooler as they neared the bay. The low hills on each side were now covered in orchards. To Nod, they seemed to go on for miles.

"Is that citrus?" Nod asked.

"Oranges, lemons, all kinds of stuff," Tom replied. "Morro Bay was all about locally grown produce."

"Why is it all still so green?"

"Probably automatic sprinklers but it could just be the air. It's always wet in this area."

"I wonder if anything is ready right now?" Nod thought aloud.

"Avocadoes, but we already have lots of those," Tom answered. "I think the citrus will be ready in a month or so. Probably some strawberries back in there somewhere."

"I wish we had time to check it out, but we're on a tight schedule," Nod lamented. He turned away from the roadside orchards just as Morro Rock, the huge boulder-looking rock formation that was a permanent feature of the landscape, came into view.

"It's still there," Nod remarked absently.

"It'll be there long after we're all gone," Clint added from the back seat.

The three large smokestacks of a long-closed power plant were also visible. To the locals, Nod was told, these tall pillars were as permanent to the landscape as the rock. A thick layer of clouds hung in the air around the bay but didn't flow onto land at this point.

"Remember ladies and gentlemen, don't use the 50's unless we get a large group attacking," Abel's voice stated over the radio. "Suppressed rifles and pistols only. There could be as many as 3,000 Crazies in the area and we don't want to meet all of them right now."

"Roger that," Tom replied through the microphone.

They continued along their predetermined route to the harbor. Nod remembered the area next to the bay. It was referred to as the Embarcadero. The main road was ringed on each side with restaurants and touristy shops. They were so close together, it was hard to tell where one building ended and another began. The boardwalk area behind the westside was where the boats were located.

As they came over the hill that overlooked the bay, Nod smiled wide. There were dozens of boats. Some were anchored on the bay while others were moored right up next to the road.

"Well, they're here," Nod commented. "That's the first question answered."

"We're turning towards the northeast side," Tom pointed out. "There may be some bigger boats by the Coast Guard area."

The boats that Nod saw closer to the shops were definitely not large yachts, though he didn't know the difference between a boat and a yacht. He suspected it had to do with the number of zeros at the end of the price tag. These were twenty to thirty foot boats. Some were fishing boats while others looked like they had been lived in at one time. Some had sails while others did not.

They continued around the edge of the bay where there were more restaurants. It was here that they encountered the first bodies. Hundreds of badly decomposed bodies littered the area close to the water where the larger boats were moored.

Nod had encountered this before. Someone who was heavily armed made their last stand here. Maybe they were trying to get to the larger boats. Nod hoped they got away.

The road continued out to Morro Rock about half a mile further. However, their first destination was at the end of the Embarcadero. The Coast Guard station was a large building that capped the end of the structures on the road.

Nod scanned the front doors. They were intact and undamaged. Could be they were locked or maybe nothing ever tried to get in. But they were heavy steel doors.

The two gunners stayed in their perches, scanning the area. Tom stayed in the driver seat while Abel was replaced by someone else in their group. Nod, Abel, Clint and Cal met up at the steel doors. All four had rifles and sidearms as well as light body armor. Those that weren't in a driver seat or gun perch stood outside the vehicles on guard.

"These doors were usually locked," Cal stated. "But keep in mind I was stationed here over 20 years ago."

"Roger that," Abel replied. He took hold of the door handle and turned. Locked. He checked the other one and found the same. "We'll head around back by the dock," he whispered. "Keep your voices down and watch each other's sixes."

"Radio check," Nod whispered into his microphone. A succession of voices came back, each replying "Gotcha." All were accounted for.

They traveled single-file along the side of the building. They weren't exactly military precision, but Nod noted they had eyes in every nook and cranny as they moved. Abel, who was in the lead, rounded the corner first and Nod saw a big smile appear on his face. When he met up with him, he smiled, too.

The Coast Guard's boat was still moored to the dock. Nod knew next to nothing about boats, but this particular one was what Cal was hoping to find. It was about ninety feet long and could comfortably hold ten people or more. It was called a 'Protector'.

"Holy shit!" Clint stage whispered. "That thing's got a '.50-Cal' on the front and back."

"As I recall, she'll make near two hundred fifty gallons of fresh water a day," Cal recalled. "That's gonna be huge."

"Okay, let's clear it first," Abel ordered. "Clint, post up here. Cal, take the pilothouse up top. Nod, you take the main deck. I'll clear below. Pistols only, fellas."

A few minutes later, the boat was cleared and all three men were in the pilothouse. Cal worked the controls to make sure everything was moving correctly, then performed the starting procedure. Finally, he put his thumb on a big, red button and stated, "Cross your fingers."

The boat made a whirring sound and Nod felt the engines fire up. The three inside and Clint on the dock nearby all raised their hands triumphantly and let out a muted yell.

"It's not as loud as I expected," Nod said.

"Until it gets throttled up, it's not bad," Cal replied. "I think the Humvees are louder." He stared at the gauges. "It all looks good to me. Diesel tanks are even full."

"Well, it's not even one yet," Abel declared. "Let's proceed as planned." He keyed his mic. "Tom, we are a go. Grab the gear and join us on the Protector. We shove off in five."

# CHAPTER 7

"It's really smooth," Tina observed. "I thought it would be, I don't know, bumpier."

"The bay is usually calm and we're moving pretty slow," Cal remarked. "Trust me, it can get bad in the open ocean."

"Is it hard to steer?" Tina asked.

"Not as long as you go slowly and remember that you're steering from the back, not the front," Cal advised.

So far, they had found six large boats that would hold six to eight passengers each. One could not be fired no matter what they tried, but it could be easily towed out of the bay and anchored, so they kept it in contention.

When they moved onto smaller boats, they decided to exclude sail boats altogether since virtually no one knew how to sail. Luckily, the more comfortable boats tended to have motors. Nod was surprised at how nice a lot of the fishing boats were and they added them to their fleet.

By the time the sun was starting to set off the Pacific Ocean, they had all of their boats picked out and lined up along the dock. The larger boats were moored on the north side near the Coast Guard facility where the docks catered to larger craft. The smaller boats were moored to the floating docks behind the shops a half mile south.

"So, Abel, what's the plan for tonight?" Nod asked.

"We'll anchor the Protector in the middle of the bay," Abel explained to everyone in the Pilothouse," Two-hour watches with two guards at a time."

"Cool," Nod agreed. "I'll take first watch at nine, so we'll all be up and going by seven a.m."

"I'll join you," Cal offered. Nod gave him the thumbs up.

"The earlier, the better," Abel explained. "We need to accomplish some goals before we head back. We got the boats, which was a big one. We checked for fuel and power and some are going to need propane or batteries for their solar arrays. Maybe a couple of hours to complete the boats."

"What else needs to be done?" Steve, one of the twins asked. His sister, Sam, smacked him on the shoulder. "I, I just mean, I thought we were only getting the boats ready."

"Yeah, what else you got in mind, Abel?" Clint asked.

"Well, a few things actually," he started. "First, there is a large grocery store up the road. Some big chain, but I don't remember which. We can check it out and maybe cut the amount of supplies we have to bring in."

"Great idea," Sophia stated.

"Thanks, Sis. Second, I think we can use The Rock as a site for placing extra fuel. That way, we don't have to chance bringing boats into the harbor and pumping it. We got lots of Jerry cans we can fill, then leave out where we can pick it up without disturbing the new 'tourists' that will be flocking to the Embarcadero."

"We can block off the road that leads out to the ocean side of The Rock," Nod suggested. "Once you get past the beach, it's a single lane road. We could push a bunch of cars on it to block it. And the area behind the breakers is above the tide line."

"That's what I was thinking," Abel told them, pointing a finger at Nod. "Steve and Sam, I want you two collecting propane bottles from the surrounding boats. Take one of the dinghies we were using today. If it's got any fuel in it, collect it. We'll check the front of the grocery store, too. Cal, Tom, Clint and Wendy will collect Jerry cans and fill 'em up with diesel. Maybe a couple with gasoline, too, but make sure you mark 'em."

"We'll collect cans from boats as we go to save time," Sam suggested, tying her long blonde hair back.

"Good thinkin'," Abel retorted. He relaxed and ran his hand through his short, thick black hair. "Nod, Sophia, Tina and me will head to the grocery store. We've been doin' it for some time, so we know what to look for."

"Don't forget sunblock," Steve stated, tying back his long blonde hair to match his sister's style. "Even if you stay below deck, you're gonna need it. Even if it's foggy."

"I hadn't thought about that," Tina admitted. "It's not usually a priority, but it needs to be now."

***

A few hours later, the boat was anchored in the bay and everyone had eaten and picked out their spots to sleep. Nod and Cal were already on deck, peering out into the darkness of town. They were surrounded by hills covered in homes and business, yet the darkness cloaked all of them. Occasionally, they could see a solar security blink on for a second or two before it sputtered out.

"You think the Crazies are setting them off?" Cal asked.

"Maybe," Nod stated. "But it could be rabbits or squirrels, too. We made a lot of noise today and no one saw a single Crazy."

"Except the dead ones over on the bank," Cal pointed out.

"Yeah, except those," Nod accepted.

"You know what worries me about that?" Cal asked.

"What's that?"

"Whatever cut all those Crazies down was on the water. They weren't by the dock and there weren't any shell casings."

"Could you tell the caliber?"

"They were .50 cal at minimum, judging by the giant holes in the bodies. But the ammo cans on the Protector were full. Plus, they couldn't have hit them from where it was moored. Someone on a boat shot all those Crazies and didn't bother to take the guns or ammo from the Protector."

"Which means they already had something bigger and more powerful than the Protector," Nod continued. "Great, we might have a pirate problem."

"Not necessarily," Cal corrected. "They might have just wanted to come to shore and cleared a path. They may not be bad guys."

"Well, we need to let everyone know in the morning," Nod stated. "Until then, let 'em sleep."

***

"Are you sure?" Abel asked in the rising sun.

"We can't be sure," Nod suggested. "The bodies are too badly decomposed and there aren't any shell casings."

"Why would they leave ammo here?" Clint asked no one in particular.

"Could be they had plenty," Sophia stated. "Or all they could carry. Probably figured they could come back if need be."

"I just want to point out that the way those bodies were tore up, it could have been bigger than a .50 cal," Cal added.

"We don't really have time for a forensic inspection," Abel said. "Whoever it was is probably long gone anyway. If everyone's ready, let's move out."

The Protector had already been moved near the fuel station on the taller dock. Steve and Samantha shoved off the Protector's small dinghy in search of propane bottles. They planned to pick up another dinghy for the bottles and tow it.

Nod's group already had the Humvees ready to go next to the dock. They rode two in each vehicle with Nod and Tina following Abel and Sophia. The grocery store was only a few blocks up the hill, but the narrow roads coupled with the buildings being so close together worried Nod. Tina appeared to be ready for anything with her rifle barrel already sticking out of the window slightly.

"How many supply runs have you been on, Tina," Nod asked.

"Not many," she replied. "Mostly the pharmacies and doctor's offices."

"Is that why you volunteered? You want more action?"

"Is that weird?"

"Not really. You were raised in a time when life moved faster. Is the nurse thing not working out?"

"Oh no, I love it! But we aren't very busy most of the time. Nobody ever gets a cold or flu and even cuts and bone breaks just need minor tending. I've been talking to Viv about sending Dina or me out on supply runs for a while. She thinks it's a good idea."

"Like a medic or corpsman. Yeah, it is a good idea."

They rounded a corner and there was the grocery store. There were scattered vehicles in the parking lot and carts everywhere, but the store itself was intact. That was a relief to Nod because several of the grocery stores they had come across had burned down. The best explanations they had were the delis had made their own rotisserie chickens and, with no one to turn them off, they eventually started fires.

They parked the Humvees at the front doors. All four disembarked the vehicles and scanned the area. Lots of windows facing the sun so it shouldn't be dark inside, Nod thought. No broken windows, so it hadn't likely been looted.

Abel entered first, forcing the sliding doors open. They stayed open behind him as Tina entered next. Sophia followed with Nod watching behind them as he moved inside. He bumped into Sophia, then turned to see why she wasn't advancing. His gaze fell on what appeared to be every bit of non-perishable food and other sundries stacked neatly at the front of the store.

"What am I looking at?" he asked.

"I think…everything," Sophia answered.

"Why…?" Tina began then stopped realizing they all had the same question.

"It's all covered in dust," Abel determined. "It's been stacked up for a while. Maybe a group came through, then got attacked and had to take off?"

"But do we take it?" Nod stated. "I mean, is this like calling 'dibs'?"

"They didn't attempt to hide it or lock it up," Sophia pointed out. "I say it's fair game."

"I'm with Sophia on this," Tina agreed. "It's been here a long time. No reason to let it all go bad."

"Alright," Abel said, throwing his hands up.

It took over an hour to load the food. It was mostly canned items along with crackers and dried pasta. After filling the backs of the Humvees, Nod noticed a large rack of propane bottles off to the side of the doors. Nod broke the lock off and they determined that six were completely full, while twelve others had been almost empty. They strapped them to the roof and started back.

Nod felt less uneasy this time. The drive back used the same route as before and nothing seemed amiss. Then he heard the gunshots. Lots of them and he followed as Abel sped up.

As they drove down the main road along the docks, they could see Crazies streaming out between the shops on the east side of the road. And they were headed right at the fuel station where the Protector was anchored.

"Tina, can you fire the .50 cal?" Nod asked excitedly.

"No, but I can drive," she replied.

Nod slammed on the brakes and got out, closing the door behind him. He jumped into the back and shimmied up through the turret. At the same time, Tina dove into the driver seat and gunned it forward. Nod charged the gun and began firing at the running Crazies.

He had done this many times and had learned to take an extra second to aim instead of spraying and hoping he hit something. His measured shots hit a different target with each round, wasting as little as possible. Between him and Sophia in the other Humvee, they were making short work of the onslaught.

When all of the attackers were down, they pulled the Humvees up to the fuel station. It had been obscured by the bend in the road until they got there. Clint was standing at the mounted gun on the front of the boat facing the road. The rest were on the dock, where someone was down.

When the four got to the end of the dock, they found Cal on one knee holding Wendy's bloody body against him. He had her hand in his, squeezing tight. Tom stood over them, his rifle up in the ready position.

"What happened?" Abel asked, his eyes scanning the dying mound of Crazies.

"They came from the shops first," Tom started, his breathing stopped by him swallowing hard. "Four of them came right through the window and headed at Cal. Wendy jumped on them, stabbing with her knife. By the time we reacted, they had already taken chunks out of her. Then they just started pouring out of everywhere from across the street. Clint was on deck and mowed 'em down with the .50. If you guys hadn't got back when you did…" He shook his head and swallowed hard again.

Tina was checking out Wendy's wounds, trying to get the larger bites and cuts covered in hopes the bleeding would stop. It was obvious to all of them that it was too late, but she wouldn't slow down.

"Why'd you do that, girl?" Cal whispered in her ear. Cal's short, red beard was matted with his tears.

She weakly answered, "You're the only boat pilot." She blinked her eyes several times. "I'm just a mommy with no kids. It's…better…like this." She closed her eyes a final time.

"Dammit!" Cal yelled. He looked to Tina, who had stopped working. She shook her head at Cal and wiped her eyes. Cal dipped his head next Wendy's and sobbed in her hair.

A few minutes later, Nod heard the sound of a small boat. He looked out on the bay and saw Steve and Sam trolling towards them, although he initially confused them since they looked so similar. Sam steered the rudder from the back with her pistol in her other hand. Steve stood half-crouched at the bow with his rifle at the ready. They towed two smaller boats loaded with white propane bottles and small solar panels.

Nod gave them a wave, then walked over to help them tie off at the lower dock. Seeing him moving slowly, Steve sat his rifle down. The look on Nod's face let them know something bad had happened. Steve tossed the mooring line to him.

"They attacked right before we got here," Nod explained, tying off the line. "We fought them off, but Wendy didn't make it. She sacrificed herself to save Cal."

Sam put her hand to her mouth and pain radiated out of her wide eyes. Steve moved to comfort her and held her close. He looked up at Nod.

"Sam was helping her," he explained. "She used to be a therapist and hoped she could do some good. And she did. Wendy lost her husband and three kids but she was starting to open up again."

"You guys take your time," Nod replied. "Join us when you can."

They debated on whether to bury her or take her body back with them. It was Sam that noticed the overgrown playground nearby and they decided it would be a good place for her eternal rest. They dug the grave, Sam said a few words and they buried her. It reminded Nod of how things were at the beginning of the outbreak, with no time to mourn properly. They had only lost two people in the last year and they had days to mourn each. Now, they had to move on quickly.

Steve and Sam had found dozens of full or nearly full propane bottles. Each could provide a boat many weeks of cooking ability. Combine that with the full tanks Nod had found at the grocery store and they had enough for many months.

The solar panels were for a different purpose. Most of the larger boats had small water desalinators that were powered by the boat motor. They would provide plenty of fresh water, but it would require them to run the motors for hours each day, which would use all the fuel they had in a few weeks.

A half dozen of the smaller boats had portable, solar powered water desalinators that only required sunlight. They made less fresh water, but since they worked all day, it would be plenty. However, they had to be installed properly, so Steve asked if he and his sister could stay there and install them and maybe look for a few more in the marina further up the bay.

Abel wasn't keen on leaving them alone, especially after they had been attacked. Cal, whose face still showed the sadness Wendy's sacrifice, stepped in and offered to stay as well. He could be their lookout while they worked. And they could all three distribute some of the food that had been loaded onto the Protector's deck onto the other boats. Abel asked the group if anyone objected and no one did.

Just after lunch, they pulled away in the Humvees. Abel, Sophia and Clint on the lead with Tom, Nod and Tina following behind. The plan was to be back the following day or the next at the latest.

The ride home was uneventful. Nod rode in the turret the entire time as did Clint in the lead truck. He was mesmerized by the chilled air off the coast. As they got further away, the air got warmer and dryer. The trip took an hour or so, with radio contact the last twenty minutes.

The Humvees pulled up to the Miller ranch which had become the supply hub. Dean had been collecting flatbed trailers and large trucks and parking them in the large pasture since the beginning. They were making use of them all now.

After a tearful reunion in which Bob Floss offered a few more words and prayers for Wendy, they quickly got back to work. Nod walked around the two flatbed trailers loaded with supplies. There were dozens of boxes all marked with their contents with everything imaginable.

"The tough part is the lack of refrigeration and freezers," Sadie said from behind him. "I know the boats probably have them, but we don't want to run the motors too much. Everything has to be dried and canned. We're actually running out of canning jars. And the meat is being turned into jerky now."

"Man, I forgot about the meat," Nod stated remorsefully. "No fresh meat other than fish for a while. What about all the cattle?"

"We slaughtered all we could. The Hightower's are gonna take some along with the horses and we'll just release the rest and hope we can recover some later to restart the herd."

"Crazies will probably get most of 'em," Nod lamented. "Chickens will probably get away, though, the little bastards."

"Bob Floss is grilling a ton of meat tonight," Sadie said with enthusiasm. "May as well gorge ourselves while we can."

***

"You gave him some of your spice rub, didn't you?" Nod asked. He sat back in his folding lounge chair, patting his full belly.

"He asked for the recipe, but I gave him a plastic jar of it instead," Sadie replied weakly as she unbuttoned the top of her pants and reclined similarly.

"I don't think I've ever eaten so much," Tex added from the hammock he occupied. "Did you pack some for Millie?"

"Yeah," Sadie assured him. "And breakfast, too."

"Oof," Nod added. "I can't think about breakfast yet."

Bob walked over from the grill, a huge plate of meat in one hand and a beer in the other. "This peanut butter IPA

102

goes well with goat," he mused. "That boy was ahead of his time."

Realizing the flippant tone, Bob darted his eyes over to Sadie. He began to fumble an apology, but Sadie smiled weakly and put her hand up. "You're right, he was."

"This whole thing is going to be so much tougher without him," Nod stated, his hand taking hold of Sadie's.

"Tough is who we are, now," Sadie replied, putting her head on Nod's shoulder.

# CHAPTER 8

Nod woke early the next morning to the sound of loud footsteps. Shaking the cobwebs, and minor hangover, out of his head, he sat up and listened. He thought he heard the loud, excited talking and a voice on the radio, but he was still foggy. A sudden pounding on the door cleared the fogginess immediately.

Nod leaped out of bed and bounded towards the door. "What is it?" he yelled.

Viv stood at the door, worry all over her face. "They're here!"

"Who's here?" Nod replied.

"The Horde, the Crazies, whatever you want to call them!" Viv said excitedly.

"Here?" Nod asked incredulously.

"The Abrams Ranch," she explained, almost breathless. "They attacked them this morning. Luckily, they had a couple of guards posted. One of them didn't make it. But they had their trucks loaded already and they're all on their way to the Millers place."

Nod was suddenly very happy he had driven home instead of staying with Sadie last night. "Shit! If they're already at the Abrams Ranch, they're already at Atascadero. We'll have to take the alternate route through Paso Robles."

"Get dressed and I'll get Lizzy ready," Viv ordered. "We're already packed, so we can leave as soon as you're good."

Nod hurried and grabbed what he hadn't already packed as he dressed. He took a second to glance at the clock on the wall and saw it was barely 5:30. All the groups had decided to pack the day before so they could leave bright and early, but the caravan was going to leave the Abrams Ranch around 9. This just threw a wrench into that idea.

Grabbing his backpack and rifle last, he headed for the kitchen door. He saw that Viv had already grabbed the radio and had Lizzy strapped into the Humvee. He closed the door and checked it was tight, then jumped off the porch and ran to the Humvee.

The back compartment was packed with their personal items and he added his backpack. Viv reached out and grabbed his rifle and placed it in the floorboard between her legs. "I'm glad we took the medical supplies and canned stuff over yesterday," she noted.

"Well, someone's looking out for us for sure," Nod added.

They stopped outside the fence and Nod closed and locked the gate. He double-checked the lock with a quick tug, then paused to look around. He thought of this old house as home and might never see the place again. He felt his throat tightened up slightly.

"It'll be here when we get back," Viv assured him from the Humvee. "Crazies don't usually 'pillage' a place."

"Did you just say 'pillage' out loud?" Nod said with a laugh.

Viv laughed, too. "It seemed to fit."

It took only a few minutes to get to the Miller Ranch. Bob Floss' group had their trucks and trailers lining the road outside the tall chain-link fence and Nod parked in line with them. Bob met Nod as he approached the gate.

"We sent up one of those long-distance drones you gave us," he started. "Shelly, she's one of the new people in our group, is really good at flying it. She flew it all the way to Atascadero. It's swamped, Nod. The Horde is there and it's moving faster than we thought. She took it up towards Paso Robles, but it died near Templeton. The Crazies were almost there."

"Damn! Hwy 46 is just a few miles north of Templeton," Nod noted, rubbing his forehead. "How long ago was that?"

"About ten minutes," Bob recalled. "Sorry, we lost the drone."

"Don't give it another thought, Bob. That was valuable intel and I've got four more drones already packed. But we gotta go now if we're gonna make it."

The two entered the residence and found all the Millers ready to go in the kitchen. "We just heard from Cindy Abrams," Tex said. "They're taking the backroads to Hwy 46. She said we better not wait for them if we don't see them there."

"You guys all ready?" Nod asked.

"Yep, we've got the Humvee packed and Millie and Trinity are already in there," Sadie assured him.

"Then let's go!" Nod urged.

The caravan consisted of an assortment of Humvees and large trucks with fully-loaded flatbed trailers. They had thought about using semi-trucks but decided against it because they weren't as fast or as maneuverable as the smaller trucks and flatbeds. Viv and Lizzy had transferred to the large farm truck that Nod felt was even better built than his Humvee and was certainly more comfortable. The trucks were not to stop for anything while the Humvees kept them secure.

Nod had Clint and Dina Floss with him. Clint was up top manning the .50 cal while Dina sat in the back seat ready to fire from either side, if necessary. They were positioned at the end of the caravan. As they neared Paso Robles, Nod picked up the radio.

"For all the drivers, remember to stay on the route we've cleared on the 101. Don't stop unless you absolutely have to." He noticed a lot of hands sticking out windows with their thumbs in the air.

Using a route they had cleared over the last couple of years, it didn't take long to reach their first destination. The off-ramp for Highway 46. The 46 would take them all the way to the coast if they followed it, but they would end up way north of Morro Bay. Luckily there was a back road that cut south towards Morro Bay. Only a handful of their group remembered this back road and they couldn't find it on a map, but those that had used it, including Bob Floss, were positive it was there.

Most of the caravan had exited onto the 46 when Nod noticed a large group of Crazies coming their way from the south. Then he realized this was only the beginning of a much larger group coming over the rise on Hwy 101.

"Heads up, everyone," Nod reported over the radio. "I think the Horde is here."

The caravan picked up speed as every vehicle was now on the 46 headed west. There were a few homes and businesses dotting the area and a large shopping center south of them. At first, Nod had seen a few dozen Crazies. Quickly that number rose to the hundreds and maybe even a thousand as they spotted the large group of vehicles. They began running impossibly fast, cutting across the shopping center towards them.

"More speed!" Nod exclaimed.

"Nod?" the voice of Bob Floss came over the radio.

"Yeah?"

"We can't let them follow us, you know. They'll keep coming. Maybe even the whole Horde will come this way."

"You're right," Nod replied. "Is there a bridge or something where we can block the road?"

"About three miles up the road there's a place where there's a cliff on one side and a steep mountain on the other," Bob explained. "Last time I came through there I saw some boulder precariously perched on the side of the mountain. A couple hundred rounds from a .50 might be enough to knock 'em down."

"Well, let's get there fast so we have a few minutes," Nod instructed. "You guys keep going and we'll try to block it."

"10-4," Bob replied.

Nod stopped a few hundred feet beyond the boulders. Bob was right, they were precariously perched fifty feet above. Nod pointed to the cluster of rocks and Clint smiled and opened fire. Hearing some ricochet, Nod and Dina took shelter behind the Humvee. Clint continued to fire bursts for a full minute, before stopping.

"They aren't moving!" Clint exclaimed. "Dammit, what's keeping them up there?"

"Well, we can use the Humvee to block the road," Nod suggested. "That'll slow them enough that maybe they'll give up. I'll have someone come back and pick us up."

Nod picked up the radio. "This is Nod. Can one of you Humvees come back for us? We're gonna block the road with our car."

He waited thirty seconds before repeating himself. No one responded. He tried a third time and still nothing.

"These stupid hills are blocking the signal," Clint explained.

The radio crackled a little and he heard a voice. "Say again," Nod asked.

"I said we're not far from you," a female voice yelled into the radio.

"Holy shit!" Dina exclaimed. "Look!"

She pointed east where they had been earlier. The Horde or at least a small part of it, was roughly a mile from them and closing fast. However, coming up the road with no regard for the lives of the Crazies was the biggest pickup truck Nod had ever seen. Maybe it was a monster truck, he thought to himself. It had a large metal scoop on the front that looked a lot like the ones trains had to move cattle off the tracks. Bodies were flying through the air or disappearing under the tires at an alarming rate. Behind it, three more trucks with trailers and a Humvee barking ordinance were headed toward them.

"This is Cindy," the voice continued. "I'm in the lead truck with Sophia. I assume you're trying to block the road.

Our last vehicle will stop to pick you up after we come through."

"Copy that," Nod replied sheepishly. He was fixated on what the truck was doing to every soft thing it encountered. Soon, it rolled past them as did the rest of the convoy. The last vehicle, a Humvee, didn't stop until it was one hundred fifty feet up the road.

Nod motioned for the other two to go meet them while he moved their rig to block the path. It blocked most of it, but the more determined would eventually get by. Nod ran to meet the waiting Humvee. Tom Abrams was waiting beside the vehicle with a long metal tube in his hands.

"It ain't gonna stop 'em, is it?" he asked.

"Probably not for long," Nod stated.

"Let's see if we can help a little more," Tom said. He stepped over a few feet and put the tube on his shoulder.

"Is that an RPG?" Clint asked.

"Yep," Tom replied, as he fired upward toward the mountain. The grenade shot out like a rocket and hit the base of the boulders causing a large explosion of tiny rocks and dirt. The boulders shook unsteadily, then began to slide and roll. Nod would have sworn half the mountain side came with them and it took only a few seconds for them to smash on the road below. Boulders of every size now blocked the path with no way around.

The radio crackled. "Did you just use our last RPG?" Abel asked angrily.

Tom walked back to the truck and picked the microphone. "Had to be done, bro. The Humvee wasn't blocking the whole road."

"All right, all right, just catch up," Abel conceded.

Inside the Humvee was a tight fit. It already had four passengers and their gear. Adding three more with their gear wasn't comfortable, to say the least. Tom's front passenger, whom Nod didn't know, gave his seat to Nod. When they were back on their way, Nod spoke.

"So, what's up with that behemoth in the front?"

"Ah, you noticed Sophia's toy?" Tom smiled.

"I've never seen that one," Nod pointed out. "Where did you get it?"

"We've been working on it a while. One of our departed neighbors used to build Monster Trucks. He has a ton of parts but only one actual truck. I think it was one of his first because it's not a full sized one."

"Coulda fooled me," Clint said from the back seat.

"Sophia really put in a lot of work. Reinforced everything, roll cages, even that cow-catcher on the front. It's a beast, for sure. We got caught behind the Horde back there and she ran over them like gravel. I hate to see what the bottom looks like, though."

When they got to the turn off that would cut back to Morro Bay, the rest of the Caravan was waiting. Nod radioed as they approached and explained what had happened. He could feel Sadie shaking her head through the radio.

They continued on a road that was poorly maintained even before the virus. Cindy Abrams, whose vehicle was the tallest, attempted to radio the group left at the bay. After trying for a few minutes, they got a reply.

"Glad you guys are close," Cal responded. "We've been seeing the Crazies build up all morning. There's not a ton yet, but it seems like more and more every hour."

"What's our best angle of approach," Cindy asked.

"Just come up the Embarcadero towards the Rock. That's the only way in and we've cleared out everything close by. Once you roll up, me and Steve will block the road with two cars while Tina and Sam cover us. But we won't have a lot of time to get the supplies and people onto the Protector and the party boat."

"Party boat?" Cindy questioned.

"You'll see it when you get here," Cal remarked.

The road dead-ended at Hwy 1, which they followed south a few miles to Morro Bay. The cars hadn't been cleared but the traffic had been light when the virus hit. A few minutes later they pulled onto the road that split the Embarcadero next to the bay.

"Flatbeds pull up closest," Nod instructed. "There's enough room for the Humvees to circle around and build a perimeter." Again, the hands hung out the windows with the thumbs up.

Nod noticed a lot more Crazies this time. Most were taken out easily, but he worried about those they didn't see. Last time, they all hid until the opportune time. These new ones were not as coordinated in movement or actions.

Two cars pulled across the road behind them when they passed a narrow part of the road. Nod saw Cal and Steve jump out and start running along the boardwalk. Tom slowed to provide them support, if needed.

When they reached the tall harbor where the Protected was moored, the flatbeds were already being offloaded. Intermittent rifle fire was going off all around them as Crazies made attempts to climb onto the road. Nod got out to help load but they seemed to have a good handle on it, so he took a position nearby, firing at Crazies as they appeared.

It took ten minutes to get all the supplies on the Protector. People were scrambling to get their personal gear out of the truck and Humvees when Nod noticed movement out of the corner of his eye. Behind the shops that were right on the edge of the bay, dozens of Crazies began to pour out on the road and boardwalk.

"Contact!" Nod yelled. "On the boardwalk!"

"Get the Protector away from the dock," Abel shouted. "Get as many people on as you can but go now! We'll follow."

"Steve's got the party boat ready on the other end of the dock!" Cal yelled back. "It'll hold twenty-five people, but it's slow!"

"Copy that!" Abel replied. "Fall back slowly, guys. Don't let them overrun us."

Nod, who somehow was the furthest away, began to back up. He had seen the party boat because it was behind the National Guard building. The Crazies kept flowing at them, working their way onto the dock now. The path was only five feet wide, but they were coming so fast it was hard to stop them.

"Steve! Start pulling away! They'll have to jump for it!" Cal yelled over the radio. The Protector was a good thirty feet from the dock, well outside the Crazies jump range. Someone on board began spraying the Crazies with the small canon. The splintered wood posts and slats began to buckle under the weight of the Crazies. And the handful of people still making their way to the party boat.

The dock began to sway under Nod's feet. He paused to get his balance and three Crazies were almost on him. As he brought his rifle up, they were dropped by someone behind him. He turned and found himself alone on the dock so he ran full out towards the party boat, which was twenty feet from the dock and almost eight feet below. He leapt with all he had and hit the back end, three people grabbing at him so he didn't fall backward.

The party boat turned out to be a large pontoon boat a local company used to ferry vacationers on 'booze cruises' just outside the bay. It was bare bones with a large, flat floor, a couple of rows of benches and a bar. The top was covered canvas and fake thatch for a south pacific theme. The twenty or so people fit on it easily.

"Would you like a beer, Nod?" Tom asked him, a cold one pointed in his direction.

"It's only nine a.m.," he replied. "Oh, what the hell. It's gonna be a long day."

# CHAPTER 9

Cal and the siblings (they hated being called twins), Steve and Samantha, had been busy the previous day. They had managed to pilot all of the boats to an area a mile southwest of the bay. The large sandbar that created the western side of the bay blocked any view of them from the mainland. The Rock was easily in sight at all times.

They had created three separate 'encampments' of boats. The Protector and the large fishing boat were anchored separately but within sight of everyone else. The 'encampments' each contained a couple of large yachts, a couple of smaller yachts and a mishmash of smaller boats for couples.

The Miller group, including Nod, Viv and Lizzy, took the smallest encampment. With several small boats left over, they were moved into the other groups. Tex took a boat for himself as did Millie for her and Trinity. Viv decided to use the larger yacht as a floating hospital. She would stay there and Tina and Dina could come when needed. All of the medical supplies were stored in the extra cabins. Nod and Sadie took the smaller yacht.

The large fishing boat, which easily held eight people, was used by a mixture of group members, most of which were couples. They planned to utilize the boat weekly for its intended purpose. They just had to learn how to use everything, which ex-Navy man Bob Floss promised to help with.

The Protector would have a floating crew. Cal would be stationed there permanently and given the Captain's cabin. Many had already started referring to him as 'Captain Cal', which made him smile. Steve and his sister Samantha would rotate duty there every other week. Six to eight others would rotate onboard weekly.

The party boat ended up being a large boon. Instead of cluttering the Protector's decks with boxes of extra supplies, they were moved there. Still, there was lots of room to walk around, so it was decided that the younger kids could be brought over regularly to 'run wild' for a while.

The first day at sea was exhausting for everyone. Loading and unloading the boats, figuring out how everything worked, including the water desalinators, and getting their sea legs wore even the strongest of them down. By the time the sun set, most people were already asleep.

Nod sat on the deck with his feet dangling over the edge. The sun was disappearing behind the water, cascading rays of light filling the overcast skies. It was the most beautiful sunset he could remember and it depressed him. His head dipped down to gaze at the water instead.

"I know who you're thinking about," Sadie stated, walking up behind him. She handed him a warm mug of hot chocolate and sat down next to him.

"Same person as you, I bet," he responded, putting an arm around her.

"He would have hated this. Being on the water, I mean," she clarified. "He hated the ocean."

"I was never a big fan of the open water, either," Nod agreed. "But it's saving our necks, so cheers." He raised his mug in the air and Sadie followed suit. "It's definitely colder here, though." He sipped his warm drink.

"Would you marry me?" Sadie asked.

Nod hesitated a second, then replied, "Like, ever, or right now?"

"I know it seems almost outdated now, but we are actually living together."

"I didn't know you were so prim and proper, Miss Sadie." Nod nudged her jokingly and they both chuckled.

"I'm serious, now. Will you marry me?"

Nod sat his mug down and took her hands in his. "I would be delighted if you would make an honest man of me," he declared.

"Okay, then. I'll find someone to marry us tomorrow," she decided. "I guess Cal's a Captain, right? Can't sea Captains do it?"

"Or Bob Floss. He was a Deacon or something. I don't know, does it really matter who pronounces us 'Man and Wife'?"

"You mean 'Woman and Husband'. I asked you, remember?" Nod shrugged and put his hands up in submission.

They sat hand and hand and stared off as the sun finally disappeared completely. "What about Tex?" Nod asked. "Will he be okay with it?"

"Tex has wanted us to get married for a long time," she replied. "He'll be fine. I'm not sure how Millie will react."

"She seemed better today."

"Yeah, well, she was really busy. That certainly helps."

"Can I ask you what made you decide to ask? Don't tell me it was the living arrangements."

"No, not really. When I put Lizzy to bed just now, she asked me if I would be her mommy. I said yes."

Nod's eyes began to tear up and he casually wiped them and looked away. "It's okay, silly. You can be emotional," Sadie stated.

"It's just that, now I know you only want me for my daughter," he fake cried.

"Ya gotta admit, she's a big plus."

"Indeed."

"Of course, if we get married, you'll have to tell me your last name," Sadie remarked.

"I told you, it's Lake."

"That's Viv's last name, not yours." Her formerly playful tone started to sound serious.

"Well, I told you a long time ago I'd let you know if you guessed it right."

"Ugh, I can't play that game anymore." Sadie tossed one hand in the air.

"Then we'll just use your last name. Everyone calls us the Miller group anyway."

"Fine," Sadie capitulated.

\*\*\*

The next morning, Sadie and Nod told Tex and Millie of their plan to wed that day. Both were overjoyed and the news seemed to perk up Millie even more. Using the radio, they asked Bob Floss to perform the ceremony and he agreed. Since there was no privacy on the radio, everyone knew about their plan. With the party boat anchored in the middle of the circle of boats, they decided to have the ceremony there.

Since there was so much work to be done on their second day at sea, they couldn't take a lot of time to plan. They just paddled over to the party boat at three p.m. and met Bob Floss and a few others. Since the boats were so close, most people could see the ceremony easily from their decks. Bob used a radio to broadcast their words so everyone could hear, too. When he pronounced them 'Woman and Husband', per their request, several people fired off shots into the air before being reminded they shouldn't be making too much noise.

That night, Viv took Lizzy back to her boat. She had made a room for her on the medical boat anyway and insisted the child go with her for a few days while Nod and Sadie were on their 'honeymoon.' Nod reminded her they weren't going anywhere, but Viv just laughed and walked away, Lizzy in tow.

While they certainly had a nice evening, the next morning brought their first big issue. When Nod came above deck, he noticed the medical boat was overwhelmed with people being seasick. Some had thrown up so much, they were dehydrated and Viv had to add some electrolytes to water and try and get them to swallow it. She had a supply of IV saline but didn't want to use it unless there was an emergency.

Nod used their small inflatable dinghy to row over and see what the problem was. It didn't take long for him to figure it out. While Tina and Dina helped make people comfortable above deck, Nod pulled Viv to the side.

"What can you do for them?" he asked.

"Not much, I'm afraid," Viv replied. "I do have some pills for motion sickness I've given to the young ones, but mostly you just have to get over it. Eventually, your body will get used to the constant movement."

124

"Do you think the enhancements the virus has made to us might help?" Nod suggested.

"I would expect it to, but who knows. Nobody wears glasses anymore or gets the flu. Shoot, I don't even have arthritis anymore. But, then again, Bob Floss' artificial hip is still there and Sophia still has a huge scar on her back from a dirt bike accident when she was twelve. The effects are not 100% predictable."

As Nod was leaving, a small group was approaching in a similar inflatable dinghy. He moved his boat from the lower deck so they could get to it. He heard someone moaning from the floor of the boat.

"Someone seasick?" Nod asked.

"Nope, ol' Curly broke his ankle," a young man replied. Nod didn't know anyone in the small group personally but did know they were with the Abrams family.

"How'd he do that?" Nod asked.

"Tried to jump to another boat from his," the young man answered. "He thought it would be easy since it was only about ten feet. He didn't think about the wet deck. He slipped and fell five feet to the lower deck. Landed wrong, I guess."

The two other guys were lifting Curly, who indeed had curly red hair, onto the boat. Nod saw the ugly twist to the ankle and shuddered. "Well, let me know if he needs anything more."

"We'll do," the young man stated.

Nod noticed a few people gathered on the party boat, including Bob Floss, who motioned for him. A few minutes later, he stepped on the deck. There were some benches along the edge and a few fold-out camping chairs had been brought over. Nod took a seat on the bench directly across from Bob, who sat in a camp chair with a steaming mug.

"You made some coffee?" Nod asked jokingly.

"I've got enough personally to make one pot each day for ninety days," he said. "After that, I can't vouch for anyone's safety." The half dozen people assembled all chuckled. He pointed to a small group of kids using a small pop-up tent as a fort. "I'm so glad they found this boat. It's still gonna be hard on the rugrats, but having this space really helps."

"No doubt," Nod agreed.

He pointed his mug towards the medical boat. "Are all those people seasick?"

"Most of them. I guess someone broke their ankle jumping from boat to boat."

"I was worried about that," Bob replied, shaking his head. "Some of these young folks think they're indestructible now. The worst thing about boats is not the constant swaying. You get used to that and even miss it a little when you get back to dry land. Nope, the worst thing is the constant dampness. Every time you get dry you end up getting splashed or step in a puddle or it rains. Every time. Takes a lot longer to get used to that."

Pete, the agriculturalist, was sitting on the end of the bench with his dog, Crowley, at his feet. "Well, I doubt we would get skin cancer, so that's a plus with all this exposure."

"True," Nod agreed, then changed the subject. "Has anyone tried to get at land yet?"

"Not that I'm aware of," Bob replied. The rest shook their heads, too.

"I wonder if the town has been swamped with Crazies?" Nod mused.

"I guess we could row over to the sandbar and take a peak over it?" Pete suggested.

"Doesn't the sand bar link up with dry land somewhere?" Nod asked.

"Yeah," Bob answered. "But it's probably four limes south and the area where it touches is pretty remote. I don't see any reason there would be Crazies on it."

"Let's do it then," Nod said. "You up for it, Pete?"

"I'm totally up for it, let's go! Should we bring weapons?"

Nod felt his side and realized for the first time he wasn't armed. He was startled by it. Then he laughed.

"What is it?" Bob asked, already starting to laugh himself.

"I just realized I'm not wearing my pistol. I can't remember the last time I didn't have it on me. It's just been like a reflex to put it on every morning."

"Enjoy it while you can," Bob chuckled.

"Well, let me grab my pistol and a rifle for you and we'll go," Nod stated.

Leaving Crowley for the kids to play with, the two men rowed back to Nod's boat where he got his weapons and let Sadie know what he was up to. Then they were on their way east towards the sand bar. Nod wasn't sure if it technically was a sandbar, but that's what everyone called it. It was more like a long hill of sand that blocked the bay. Being only a mile or so out, they could see it most of the time. But it was tall enough that even the Protector, at least twenty feet above water at its highest point, couldn't see over it.

The current was different as they got closer. Nod, who was paddling now and Pete would paddle back, fought the current to stay in the right direction. It took twenty minutes to get there and Nod's arms and shoulders were on fire.

"Boy," he said rubbing his shoulders. "I can't remember aching this much in a long time."

"Great," Pete replied. "Hope the current shifts before we go back."

After a few minutes of climbing, they summited the top of the sand. Both relaxed on their stomachs and took out their binoculars. They didn't need them. There were thousands of Crazies shuffling along the streets of Morro Bay. Their general direction of movement was north, but just as Nod had seen when they flew over LA, there were pockets moving in other directions, too. The area in front of the Coast Guard building had hundreds of Crazies walking in circles as there was only one road in and out. The whole town was swamped.

Nod was looking through his binoculars at the boardwalk when he noticed a few Crazies had stopped and were looking out their way. It took a few seconds for him to realize what they were looking at.

"Shoot! Slide down," he stage whispered.

Pete did as instructed. "What was it?" he asked.

"Six or seven Crazies staring right at us," Nod explained. They had rolled to their backs now.

"Toward us or at us," Pete asked.

"I think they spotted us and knew what we were," Nod clarified.

"Well, I guess that makes sense," Pete explained. "They aren't the decaying monsters we always saw in the movies. Other than their clothes rotting off, they're probably in as good a shape as we are, vision included. Hell, I used to wear Coke-bottles myself."

"Me, too," Nod revealed.

"So, we really do need to stay out of sight until they pass," Pete reaffirmed.

"Yep," Nod agreed. "Probably shouldn't be too loud either. Although the waves probably cover most loud noises."

"Sound actually bends towards the water, too," Pete stated. "It doesn't travel very far."

"What?" Nod asked with a chuckle.

"I know, I know, weird information," Pete said, putting his hand up. "I spent twelve years in academia, man. Cut me some slack. My head is filled with maybe 25% useful information and the rest is little more than weird trivia."

"Are you kidding me? That kind of 'weird' information is the stuff of survival now."

They lay there looking up at the clouds for a moment in silence. Nod had a question he kept meaning to ask Pete and finally had the time.

"Do you think the crops are going to make it, Pete?" he asked without looking at him. "You know, this evacuation is going to deplete our stock of scavenged and preserved food. I want to know what to expect when we return."

Pete thought for a few seconds. "There's just too many variables. If everything goes 100% our way, we'll return in a couple months to a bountiful harvest."

"And if it doesn't?"

"Well, the irrigation is completely automatic. We did our best to bury all the lines before we left, but if thousands of Crazies traipse through the field, it may destroy the water lines and the crops. We got as much fertilizer in the soil as we could when we planted, so that should be good. But even if they avoid the fields completely, there's bugs and weeds and varmints to deal with. All the things we'd be taking care of daily if we were there."

"Bottom line, if they don't destroy the fields and the irrigation stays on?"

"Probably 50% reduction in crop yield. Still plenty enough to feed everyone. To tell the truth, I'm more worried about being back before we need to begin harvesting. Maybe two months."

"Roger that," Nod replied, turning over to make his way back to the small boat.

They paddled back to the party boat. Thanks to the current being in his favor, Pete managed to row them back in just over ten minutes. Still, he rubbed his shoulders as vigorously as Nod had when he was done.

"They're everywhere," Nod announced to the waiting group, which now included Sadie, among others.

"Are they moving?" Clint Floss asked.

"Yeah," Pete answered. "But not very quickly. And they can see very well. Nod thinks some of them noticed us atop the sand bar."

"Well, it's just confirmation of what we already knew," Bob submitted. "We just sit tight and pray that they are gone in a timely manner."

"Kinda makes you feel helpless," Sadie stated. "We're all just so out of place out here on the water. On land, there's a million things we can be doing to occupy our time. Out here, well, time is gonna pass slowly."

"It's funny," Clint noted. "A few years ago, how many people would have jumped at the chance to spend a few months at sea, no responsibilities, no jobs, just drifting and relaxing under the sun?"

"Maybe on one of the big cruise ships," Cindy Abrams added. "Lots of space on the decks. Workout rooms. Dance clubs and bars. Shows. Out here space is limited, water's too cold for swimming most of the time and we only have a few dozen DVD's and books."

"Oh, yeah," Sophia interjected. "I forgot to tell you. Dee was able to download thousands of eBooks and movies before we left. She's got tons of thumb drives filled with them. She said we should start spreading them around since everyone has laptops."

"That should help," Clint said. "Any good war movies?"

"What do you think?" Sophia said with a raised eyebrow. Clint gave her a thumbs up.

Tex's voice came over several of the radios. "This is Tex. I'm on the Protector. We've got contact with the Hightower's."

# CHAPTER 10

Cindy took her radio from her belt. "That's good news, Tex. We're heading that way, now."

They had set up a system for using the radios before they even left land. It was remarkably simple. There was a channel designated for the group 'leaders' and another for general info. Most of the boats were in yelling distance, and most people didn't want their radios squawking every few minutes but they wanted something for important announcements like Nod and Sadie's wedding. While anyone could tune to the leaders channel, most just kept them tuned to the general channel and relied on word of mouth for any other gossip.

Nod, Sadie, Cindy and Bob rowed over to the Protector for a briefing. The Protector, due to its size, was anchored a little further out than the other boats, but still close. It took only a few minutes to reach it.

Tex had gone over early to work with Cal. A handful of younger folks wanted to learn to pilot the boats and Cal was willing to teach them. Some stayed on the Protector full time while others, mostly those with families, came over whenever he would give a lesson. So far, they had only gone over the instruments, but it had only been a few days.

Tex and some of the others helped them aboard. Cal was holding the mic when they got to the radio.

"Hey Dan, the group leaders just arrived. Why don't you repeat what you told me," Cal spoke loudly.

"Sure, hope everything is going well for you guys. So far, we haven't seen any Crazies wandering up to the lake. We did manage to block the only road up with several barricades. Our place isn't visible from the 101, so hopefully none get the urge to explore too much."

Nod reached out to Cal and he passed him the mic. "Hey, Dan, it's Nod. Did Dale manage to get the cameras in place?"

"Hey Nod, good to hear your voice. He did get some of them up, yeah. He got one up on the road before the barricades, another on the road up here and one on the property. We didn't get the one up overlooking the 101, though, the Horde started showing up too soon."

"No worries, man," Nod replied. "I'm just glad we were able to get word to you guys before we bugged out."

"Me, too," Dan stated. "I thought we had another day for sure. We had a couple guys down near the 101 when you called. They might not have made it back if they'd been surprised by too many of them. Anyway, with the cameras up, they can't surprise us at all now."

"Ask him about the horses," Sadie whispered.

Nod smiled. "Hey, Dan, Sadie wants to know how her horses are doing?"

"We got 'em set up just north of the buildings. It's a nice little pasture area we had already put together. Some of the kids are taking turns brushing and feeding them each morning. Don't worry, we'll keep 'em safe."

"That's great news, Dan," Nod stated. "They're the last four horses in the area, I'm afraid. We turned the rest loose before we left, but I don't know if any will make it."

"That's too bad," Dan replied. "Anyway, I've got some work to do so I'm gonna get off this thing. I'll have someone nearby in case you guys need something. Just give us a holler."

"We'll do, Dan," Nod agreed. "Have a good day."

Nod handed the mic back to Cal. "Well, good news for them so far."

"What was that about cameras?" Bob asked.

"Dee had given them an internet router a while back so they could try and get to some internet servers. I guess there are a couple of computer geeks staying at the lake and they offered to help her. Since they have internet access, we gave them some of the portable cameras we built a few months ago for monitoring areas around town. Each unit has a camera, a wireless router, a battery and a solar charger. All you have to do is connect to them via the internet and voila!"

"Can we get access to those cameras?" Cindy asked.

"I don't see why not," Nod thought out loud. "We have all the specs for them. Of course, they could get smashed like the ones we left in Atascadero."

"Might be good to monitor them if we lose contact," Cindy suggested. "Maybe the Horde won't know what they are when they see them like the ones from around here."

"Yeah, they didn't last long as soon as they figured out we had left them there," Nod remembered. "But these Horde members, they don't seem as smart as the smaller groups around here. They still attack each other sometimes."

"Speaking of the internet," Sam, the female half of The Siblings, began. "I know we were getting some sporadic communication from other groups around the world a while back. Is that still going on?"

"Yeah, to a lesser degree now, unfortunately," Nod answered with sadness creeping into his voice. "We had contact with a dozen or so groups for a long time, but it's dwindled from a dozen to half a dozen in the last year. Servers go down, satellites go out of sync and groups break down." He paused to think for a second. "I think the closest group is near San Francisco. A couple of groups are doing very well in northern Canada, thanks to the extreme cold. A small group outside Spokane, Washington is very active online. Who knows how many there are that just don't have the skills to get online."

"Hopefully, a lot," Sadie suggested.

"I can't believe there is a group in San Francisco," Sam stated.

"They were lucky," Nod explained. "They're on the edge of the city. A bunch of Silicon Valley types got stuck in their high-tech building when the virus hit. The whole building is on water in San Francisco Bay. Makes its own power through solar panels. Water filters on the plumbing. They even had a huge green space area on the roof they turned into a garden. There's about a dozen of them. Only issue is the sharks."

"Sharks in San Francisco?" Sam asked.

"Yeah, I guess a lot of Crazies have fallen into the bay from the Golden Gate bridge. Enough that the shark population has noticeably increased. According to that group, anyway. There were always sharks, just a lot more now."

"That's crazy," Sam lamented, shaking her head. "Are there sharks around here?"

"Yeah," Bob replied. "Every so often there'll be a shark sighting here or Avila beach, just south of us. Pretty rare. Unless there's a food supply, they won't be coming around here much, I imagine."

***

It took two weeks for the first shark sighting to occur. The fishing boat had returned earlier in the day from its first overnight excursion. The trip was a huge success with lots of fish being caught. Most of the crew was thrilled to begin processing their harvest on the trip back, throwing the unused parts of the fish overboard as they made the ten-mile trip back to the group. They were joined by others when they arrived and soon someone noticed a fin in the water. Over the next few hours, several more fins became visible.

From then on, any larger scale fish processing had to be done a few miles out to sea. Smaller amounts were encouraged to be saved and used as bait. A few people had had some success building make-shift crab pots and the frozen fish remains made for good bait.

Sometimes Nod wasn't sure what type of fish they were eating. Vivian always seemed to have a fish stew ready to go and Nod was pretty sure she just added fresh fish to the pot each time she cooked it.

Everyone had been experimenting with the local fish and before long, someone had even made a cookbook using an old cell phone to take pictures and make notes. A few people had fished the area and knew the names of some of the fish, but a few species were a mystery until someone discovered an eBook in Dee's hastily downloaded library that helped identify the rest.

*** 

By the end of the first month, pretty much everyone's love affair with the 'fruits of the sea' had run its course. The novelty of 'tossing in a line and bringing up a meal' began to wear thin for Nod even earlier than that. He never really cared for seafood to begin with, so this was especially hard on him. Still, a few others had shellfish allergies and couldn't even enjoy the crabs or oysters.

For Memorial Day, a few of the group members decided to grill hamburgers using dehydrated ground beef they had brought. It was determined that one burger per person wouldn't deplete the food stores too much. Since there were many small grills on the boats, people could pick up their pre-formed patties and go back home or stay on the party boat and eat it there.

Peter had brought in a bunch of chips he had made from kelp. It took him several weeks to figure out, but he learned how to dry the kelp leaves just enough, then add a blend of seasoning so that the final product tasted like a chewy barbeque potato chip. Most people enjoyed them but Sadie only allowed so much to be made because it depleted the spices too much.

"Nothing like a wood-fired burger," Pete observed, taking a big bite from his sandwich.

"Well, don't get used to it," Nod suggested. "I don't think there's another piece of driftwood anywhere on this side of the sand bar. We cleaned 'em out." Nod noticed Pete actually slowed his chewing to savor what was in his mouth. "It's funny, though, I don't think I've missed food so much since this all began. I met up with Vivian so soon after and she's always had so much food, I never really felt deprived until now."

"Me and Crowley had some very lean months, unfortunately," Pete stated. He pointed to his dog who was enjoying an undercooked patty that had 'accidently' been dropped. "Ol' Crowley used to go out to find squirrels to eat while I made a can of green beans last three days. I must have looked pretty pathetic because one time he brought me back something he couldn't finish."

"What was it?" Nod asked.

"I can't say for sure. Maybe a possum or a raccoon. It was pretty messed up but smelled fresh so I cooked it. Best mystery meat I ever had."

"I wanna say that's disgusting but another week of fish chowder and I might be tempted with something like that myself." Both men laughed.

The radio on Nod's hip hissed briefly, followed by Cal's voice. "I hate to bother everyone, but there's a situation with the Hightower's."

Nod picked up his radio first. "What is it, Cal?"

"You guys, the leaders I mean, need to get over here ASAP," Cal replied. "Dan says some of the Horde shifted and might be coming at them."

"We'll be right there," Nod confirmed as he stood up. He saw Sadie, Bob and Cindy already striding towards a dingy. He followed along and rowed the hundred yards to the Protector. No one really spoke on the way.

A couple of the young volunteers helped them onto the deck. Nod saw Sophia and Dee were already there. Dee often used the Protector's equipment to access the internet since it was far better than the portable equipment she had brought along. She was busily working to access the cameras the Hightower's had put up. Two were already up on monitors and she was working on the third.

Nod grabbed the mic from Cal's outstretched hand. "Dan, what's the situation?" he asked somewhat breathless.

"Not good," Dan replied. "I noticed one of the horses was gone this morning. When I went looking for it, I tracked it moving towards the 101. Maria finally found it on the furthest camera and radioed me. She said it was coming back towards the lake. I was real happy about that, then a few minutes later she said dozens of Crazies were headed up the road. I guess they saw the horse and spooked it, so it was running home. So, they chased after it. We lost the signal to the farthest camera not long after but not before Maria saw hundreds more coming up the road."

"Damn," Nod stage whispered before keying the mic again. "Are they there yet?"

"No, the barricades are holding for now, but I think they got wind of something. They keep pushing, trying to go forward or around. Hell, maybe they can smell us up here, I don't know. Anyway, we've got the barges loaded with supplies and Dave's already floating them out to the middle of the lake. We haven't engaged them in hopes they give up and move on."

"No!" Dee yelled. "They just busted through the barricade!"

"Did you see it, Dan!" Nod yelled. "They're through!"

"I see it," Dan replied with more calm than Nod could imagine. "I need to get out there, Nod. We need to keep them off long enough to get to everyone on the lake."

"Godspeed, Dan," Nod stated, a hitch in his voice.

They all crowded in front of the monitors. They were large and hung from the ceiling along the edge of the wheelhouse. The farthest camera, showing the road up to the lake, had been smashed. It might have been purposefully done or inadvertent underneath the hundreds of feet moving quickly up the road.

The second camera showed a multitude of bodies moving past it. Dozens had been crushed at the barricade creating a ramp of dead flesh they were using to climb over effortlessly. Most barely even slowed down as they passed.

The last camera showed some of the small lodges they had used as well as the widest part of the lake. They could see several large barges piled high with boxes of all shapes and sizes and a handful of people, too. There were several more barges being pulled out to the middle, also containing boxes and people.

A skirmish line formed on the edge of the lake as people lined up to keep the Crazies back long enough for everyone to get to the barges. The distance from the camera made it hard to tell who was who, but one of the people wore a large cowboy hat similar to the one worn by Dan Hightower. There were no boats to carry them, but Nod knew they could swim for it. None of them had the chance as they were overwhelmed soon after the last barge reached the middle.

Crazies began entering the water. They lacked the motor skills to swim, so many floated or were squashed underneath the squall of bodies moving forward. Nod had been to that lake only a few times but he knew it wasn't very wide. The barges were maybe a football field away from the water's edge. The barges began to move lengthwise to get away from the Horde, but their small outboard motors were not built for speed.

The group watched in horror as the Crazies edged forward, crushing those on the leading edge. A flotilla of decimated bodies was forming, deep enough that it provided sure footing for the rest. It grew further and further until people on the barges began jumping into the water to get away. The camera cut out as the barges were overrun, sparing the onlookers from seeing the end.

Heads dropped, some in frustration, others in prayer. A few began to cry softly. Sadie grabbed at Nod and buried her face into his chest. His own eyes were teared up, but he continued staring at the blank screen.

"Maybe some got away," Dee suggested, her throat catching. "There weren't any Crazies on the other side of the lake and they'd have to go for miles to go around it." She looked at Sophia. "It's possible, right?"

"There's nowhere to go on the other side," she replied softly. "It's nothing but steep mountain on that side. They'd be on them in a few minutes." Hearing this, Dee collapsed into her, sobbing.

"Well," Bob began, blowing out a large breath. "Let's let everyone know what's happened."

# CHAPTER 11

Time passed even more slowly after what would come to be called the "Hightower Massacre." Initially there was a lot of anger towards the Hightower men for choosing to stay behind, but after most had cooled off, reason worked its way back in. Everyone had had friends in the group and the sense of loss weighed heavily.

It was two weeks later before anyone even mentioned the idea of having a small memorial for them. It was a solemn occasion, as would be expected. About half the group was on the party boat while the other half listened on the radios.

Pete, who had lived with the Hightower group for a year before moving to the Abrams group, spoke about each person. Nod was impressed at how much he knew about every individual in the group. And he managed to make it through every abridged eulogy before finally succumbing to his sadness while speaking of his good friend, Pancho. He had to take a minute to recover but he managed to finish.

That evening, Nod, Sadie and Stephanie sat on the edge of the yacht with their legs hanging above the water. Nod and Sadie ended pretty much every day like this, but Stephanie, who had been staying on the Protector most of the time, joined them this time. The sun was setting into the Pacific as they sipped on some hot chocolate.

"This is nice," Stephanie observed.

"Best thing about living out here," Sadie agreed.

"As long as the sharks don't bite your feet," Nod joked. All three chuckled.

Stephanie got serious. "You don't think they could actually…" she started.

"Probably not," Nod laughed.

"What the heck," she stated. "May as well live dangerously."

"Hey, Nod, how are we going to know when we can go back home?" Sadie asked. "We were going to rely on the Hightower's to tell us when the Horde passed."

"I suppose we'll just monitor Morro Bay and wait for it to thin out here first," he mused. "Then we can send scouts further inland."

"We're almost two months in and they don't seem to be slowing down," Sadie said. "At least not from what I've heard from you guys."

"If anything, there seem to be more," Nod admitted. "Every time we go look over the sand bar, it looks like there are more bodies. Some are moving on, but others are taking their place."

"If we had a chopper, I'd be able to see what's going on," Stephanie lamented, staring down at her cup.

"I was thinking about that the other day," Sadie interjected. "There's an airport, a small one, in Oceano, just south of Pismo Beach. It's real close to the water and I'm pretty sure it's just sand dunes between the water and airport. There might be something there you could fly."

"Yeah, it was like a tourist trap, right?" Nod remembered. "You could take planes along the coast and stuff."

"Yeah," Sadie agreed. "If we could get a chopper there, you could land it on a small island to store it. Avila is only eight or ten miles south of here and there is an island just outside the Harbor. Just a flattened piece of land, no structures."

"I read about that place when we visited," Nod said enthusiastically. "A family of whalers lived there a long time ago or something like that. Only a hundred feet across and flat as a pancake."

"What do you think, Stephanie?" Sade asked.

"If there's a chopper at that airport, it's been sitting a long time," she thought out loud. "The fuel might be good, but it would need a lot of parts lubricated first." She thought quietly for a moment, then added, "It's worth taking a look at. I'm in."

"It's risky," Nod stated, rubbing the stubble on his chin. "The only payoff is we have some aerial intel, which is huge. But we would have to glass the area, hope there's not many Crazies around. Lubing and fueling might be quiet, but as soon as it fires up, well, it's gonna be like ringing the dinner bell. And if it won't fly, we aren't likely to get very far."

"Did you say 'glass' the area?" Sadie laughed.

"It's a military term," Nod defended himself.

"Okay, Sarge," Sadie chided him. "Let's talk to Cal tomorrow and get his input."

***

"I just don't see the benefit," Cal stated. "I mean, you're only getting intel that time will give us eventually."

"We're over two months into this thing," Nod said. "We brought enough food and supplies for four months comfortably. If it's gonna be much longer than that, we're gonna need to start rationing food soon. And toilet paper."

"Don't forget the boats," Sadie added. "We've lost three to leaks since we started. Some of the water filters aren't working anymore either. We may need to sneak into the harbor just to pick up a few more of those."

Cal put his hands up. "Hey, I'm just a boat pilot. I'll do whatever you guys want. I'm just not sold on risking Stephanie's life like this."

"It's okay, Cal," Stephanie assured him. "There is no way I would try and fly anything I didn't think was fit. If we can't make it work, we'll just come back to the boat."

"You're a smart girl, Stephanie," Cal relented. "If you want to do this, I'm with you. Just let me know what you guys need from me."

"Hopefully, just a ride," Nod replied.

***

They spent several days planning for the excursion. The Protector, which hadn't gone very far at this point, would be used to transport Stephanie, Nod and a handful of others to a spot half a mile off the coastline at Oceano. Since Whaler's Island was near the Avila pier, it was between Morro Bay and Oceano so they could check that it was all clear first. If everything checked out, Nod, Clint and Stephanie would use the Protectors small dinghy to get to the beach at Oceano. They would paddle in, then Clint would use the motor to return to the Protector once the chopper, if it even existed, was in the air. They would meet up again at Whaler's Island.

The crew set off in the early morning after telling everyone goodbye. Whaler's Island was only 15 miles from their current location. The view wasn't very informative. The water's edge was mostly sea cliff until they passed by the Diablo Nuclear Powerplant. Even that small, flattened out area looked deserted. Nod figured the fail safes that prevent explosions must have worked or there would only be a crater.

The lighthouse came into view first. Nod had visited it right before the virus struck, and it looked intact. The Island was right next to it with a small jetty of rocks connecting the island to the rocky shoreline. Nod didn't see any access to the shoreline, so the island was safe for now.

"You said a family of whalers lived on the little thing?" Clint asked.

"Yeah, I'm surprised you never heard the story, living so close," Nod stated.

"That's touristy stuff," Clint explained. "My family never did any touristy stuff. All we ever did in Avila was fish or golf."

"There's plaque on the pier or harbor or whatever it is," Nod said. "Gives a little info that explains why there is an odd little flat island there. Used to have a house on it, but time and waves removed it all eventually."

As they continued on, Nod pointed to the east. "What's that long pier? Some kind of university thing, right?"

"Yeah," Cal replied. "It was run by Cal Poly. Some kind of marine research unit. It's like a mile long, only wide enough for a single vehicle to get down it. Has a building at the end where they stored stuff."

"Usually locked up tight, too," Clint added. "Big fence with big locks. Always wanted to fish off it but couldn't get to it."

The Protector continued south another ten miles. The sea was calm, as it had been all this time. The sun was out, so it was warmer than usual. Clint told Nod that, for some reason, Avila and Pismo were always warmer than Morro Bay. He didn't know why, it was just a personal observation.

Cal dropped anchor just off the shore at Oceano. Nod added three suppressed rifles and two backpacks to the small boat. The backpacks had extra ammo and a few survival supplies. Cal had his extra ammo on a chest rig attached to his belt.

The sea was a little rougher in the dinghy. Luckily, they only had to row a few minutes, before the current caught them and pulled them in. The sun was above the hills to their east now, which made Nod warm in his clothes and gear.

They pulled the dinghy up on the beach and surveyed the area. The small patch they had landed on was obscured on both sides, by design, and no one was about.

Nod put his hand to his lips. "Low tones from here on out, okay?" The other two nodded.

Stephanie and Nod began walking toward the dunes one hundred yards away while Clint stayed on the beach. The soft sand threw Nod off balance for a while, but he adapted to it pretty fast. It helped that they had visited the sandbar weekly, but they didn't walk around very much while there.

They crouched as they repeatedly walked up and over the dune hill and down the other side. It was supposed to be a short jaunt, but to Nod it felt more like a hike. He really was out of practice.

They passed a row of hedges and came to a short chain link fence. Beyond the fence, was the small runway. They both scanned the area for aircraft.

"Two small airplanes," Nod whispered aloud. "Cessna's?"

"Yeah, or at least that type," Stephanie replied. "Do you have any binoculars?"

Nod handed her his small pair. "I think I see a tail rotor. It's sticking out from behind a building."

"Let's go check it out," Nod suggested. They both climbed over the fence easily, their rifles still in their hands. They continued their crouch walk along the edge of the short runway until they got to the building. When she peeked behind it, Stephanie had a big smile on her face.

"This is perfect," she stage whispered.

"Kinda small, isn't it?" Nod suggested.

"That's what we want. It's a two seater and looks to be in great shape. Ranchers will use these to survey their cattle, but this one has pontoons on the skids. Probably a search and rescue craft." She walked over and carefully opened a side door. Fiddling with the instruments, her smile grew. "The battery's low but good enough, I think. The fuel tank is only a quarter full. If you can find a gas can and fill it up with Avgas, I'll look for a grease gun."

"Negative," Nod remarked. "We don't split up even if it takes longer."

Stephanie grimaced. "Okay, but I don't see any Crazies."

"Just a good rule of thumb when out in the wild," Nod replied.

After searching for a few minutes, they found the large tank used to refuel. They had to search the small outbuilding to find a large gas can. Stephanie suggested using a screen since, according to her, the 'Avgas doesn't really go bad, it just gets junk in it.' Nod quietly tore off the window screen and doubled it over.

It took a while to fill the gas can, so Stephanie looked around the immediate area for a grease gun. She spotted one sticking out the back of a work truck. Once the can was full, they grabbed the grease gun and walked back to the chopper. Stephanie began greasing the aircrafts many moving parts while Nod filled the chopper's tank.

It took four trips to the large tank to fill the small chopper to its limit. Each time, Stephanie had to stop what she was doing and go with Nod. In all, it took them over an hour to fill the tank and do all the preflight maintenance Stephanie felt was necessary.

They both sat in the cockpit as Stephanie began flipping switches. The thin side doors were closed but the small windows were down. Each had a pistol in their lap and their rifles squeezed between them.

"Once I start the rotors, it's gonna get loud," Stephanie explained. "Like really loud. If there's any Crazies within a couple of miles, they're gonna hear and come running. It might take a few minutes for the rotors to get up to. Or they may not get up to speed if the engine isn't tuned very well."

"How long before we know if she's going to fly?" Nod asked, his hand tightening on his pistol.

"Less than a minute, I would think," she guessed.

"Alright, then let's agree that if you're not sure at forty-five seconds, we bail and make a mad dash to the beach."

"Agreed, just remember to duck when you get out. It's not as tall as a regular helicopter."

"Thanks for the reminder."

Stephanie flipped a switch and a loud whirring sound started from somewhere above their heads. Stephanie's face pinched. Nod noticed the large rotor wasn't spinning. It was jerking.

"Something's wrong," Stephanie noted. "The rotor must be seized up! We need to bail now!"

Nod began to open the door when he spotted the first Crazy in the distance. It was maybe a half mile away but coming fast toward Stephanie's side.

"We got company!" he yelled.

"Wait!" Stephanie shouted back. "The rotor is tethered to the tail. I forgot to unhook it."

"I'll grab it, you stay here."

"You'll have to cut it and move out of the way fast. It's trying to turn and I can't shut the engine off or we'll have to start all over."

"Got it," Nod confirmed. "Listen, if they get too close, you take off. Don't wait for me, you hear me?"

"It's gonna jump up fast, Nod!" she warned. "These little ones don't lift off slowly. Just get back here!"

Nod closed the door and latched it. He took out his large knife from its holster and began sawing at the thick rope. Suddenly, it broke loose, hitting the knife and causing it to smack him in the forehead. He flew backward onto the ground.

With stars in his eyes, he managed to stand back up. The rotor whisked by the top of his head and he dropped down again. He felt his forehead and his hand came away with a little blood, but not too much. "Must have hit the flat side," he thought.

He heard a scream just over the sound of the increasingly rapid turning blades. The Crazy now had several friends joining him and they were too close for comfort. Nod crawled under the tail rotor to Stephanie's side of the chopper. He pulled his pistol and began to aim and fire slowly at each of the oncoming Crazies. The last few years had taught him to take the time to aim when you can to conserve ammo. He had ten rounds in the magazine and two more magazines on his belt.

He crouched and moved forward toward the advancing group. One had turned to four. Four had turned to a dozen. Seconds later, there were two dozen moving in fast.

He had taken down six when he had to switch magazines. As he did, he heard Stephanie yell at him. He turned and she gave him a thumbs up. He smiled and started to take a step when he quickly did the math in his head. By the time he got to the other side of the chopper, a few of these Crazies might be close enough to damage the rotors. There wasn't a big enough safety margin for him to risk getting back. He returned the thumbs up, pointed to the sky and turned to face the coming onslaught.

Although he couldn't see her, Nod knew Stephanie was hesitating. She yelled again and he gave her a backhanded wave and continued to fire. A few seconds later, he heard the chopper rise quickly into the air.

Nod changed magazines again, knowing there were more Crazies than bullets. He resolved to save the last one for himself. Nine. Eight. Seven. He paused to aim again. Six. Five. The rest were half a football field from him and he paused again to take a deep breath.

The advancing line began to fall before Nod could begin firing again. He looked behind him and saw Clint stand atop a sand dune one hundred feet away. He was looking through the scope of his rifle and sending bullets every few seconds. He raised his fist in the air when he realized Nod had seen him.

Nod ran as fast as he could toward the sand dunes. He could hear the report of Clint's rifle, but didn't dare take the time to look behind him. He bounded over the chain link fence and sped toward the sand dunes. As he neared Clint at the top of the dune, he began to slow.

"Don't slow down!" Clint yelled, turning to do the same. Nod took a half a second to look behind him and wished he hadn't. Several hundred Crazies were now behind them, some already cresting the chain link fence.

"Shit, shit, shit!" Nod yelled, picking up speed. Clint was a full dune ahead of him now and Nod wasn't moving fast enough in the soft sand to catch him. Luckily, the Crazies were all slowing slightly as their feet hit the sand, too.

When Nod summited the final dune, Clint was already at the boat, pushing it toward the water. Nod's feet hit the hard sand and he no longer felt like he was moving in slow motion.

"Duck!" Clint yelled, pulling the rifle up.

Nod dove forward and slid in the sand, then began to roll. The entire time he was moving, he heard the rifle firing and may have felt a few of the bullets as they moved only a few feet over him. Gone was the slow, measured shots Clint had made before. He was spraying now and that wasn't a good sign.

Nod heard the hard hits in the sand behind them. He knew instantly that someone was firing the .50 cal from the Protector from half a mile out. Sand and guts were exploding into the air causing enough chaos that he and Clint were able to get the boat in the water and start the engine. Both men took turns shooting anything that got too close as whoever was using the .50 cal was being careful not to get too close to them. Within two minutes, they were in water too deep for the Crazies to follow.

Nod and Clint began to laugh uncontrollably. This wasn't the first time either one of them had been so close to death, but that didn't take away the incredible relief they felt.

After the laughter died down, Nod asked, "Why were you there?"

Clint laughed again. "I was worried. It seemed like it was taking a long time. I got there right as the chopper lifted off. At first, I thought both of you were on it, then I heard your gunfire. You were too far to yell at, so I just started firing. Why were you just standing there?"

Nod half laughed. "I just didn't see the point. There were too many. Figured they would overtake me before I got back to the beach."

Clint laughed again. "Man, when you came over that last dune and then all the Crazies were right there, oh man! Did you ever see the first Indiana Jones movie, in the beginning, when he's being chased through the jungle and he comes over the hill yelling at the pilot?" They both started laughing uncontrollably again as they reached the Protector.

160

# CHAPTER 12

"Who was the sniper?" Nod asked, with sarcastic emphasis on the word 'sniper.'

Cal reached out to help him onto the deck. "Who do you think?"

"Had to be Tom," Clint suggested.

"Guilty," Tom Abrams admitted, his hands in the air. "No one else wanted to chance it since we were essentially firing over your heads. But I knew we could do it."

"You damn sure did," Nod stated, bumping fists with Tom. "I'll be spitting sand for a week, but it gave us the time we needed to get away."

"Psssh," Clint said, following up with a fist bump of his own. "Any excuse to shoot the .50." They all three laughed.

"So, we saw the chopper fly up and over towards the island," Cal recounted. "Why weren't you on it? Was it too small?"

"No, I just had to give her some fire support and we ran out of time," Nod admitted. "I'll tell you about it on the way to pick her up."

Half an hour later, they spotted the helicopter on Whaler's Island. Stephanie had been sitting in it until she saw the Protector, then got out waving her hands. Nod and Tom took the dinghy over to the island and met her. She hugged Nod tight when she realized it was him.

"I started toward the island then doubled back to make sure you made it to the beach," she recalled. "Once you were in the water, I came here. I tried using the radio to contact the Protector, but I don't think it's working."

"How'd she fly?" Nod asked.

"Smooth, for the most part," she said. "The wind definitely has more of an impact on her."

"Did you try and look for the Horde?" Tom inquired.

"No, I wanted to wait for a second pair of eyes. Should we go?"

"I'm ready," Nod replied.

"Tom, you might want to take the boat back to the Protector. It throws up a lot of water when she spins up." Tom gave her a thumbs up and started back to the boat.

Stephanie hugged Nod again. "No more of that crap, okay?" she stated. "I really couldn't take losing another f-friend."

It was unmistakable that Stephanie's slip intended another word. "Oh, Steph, that's what friends do." He gave her another tight hug, then they headed for the chopper.

\*\*\*

"We're, what, thirty miles south?" Nod asked into his headset.

"About that, if the GPS is working correctly," Stephanie affirmed.

"It's really starting to thin out here, huh?" he suggested.

"Yeah, I mean, still a lot of 'em, but you can see a lot more space between 'em," Stephanie agreed.

They continued south, watching as the density of Crazies became less and less. By the time they reached Santa Barbara, they numbered in the few hundred per mile.

"This is good news, right?" Stephanie asked. "I mean, look south and there's even less coming up the 101."

"This is great news," Nod stated. "If this is all that are coming, we probably don't have more than a couple weeks until it's mostly clear. Three tops. Are we okay on fuel?"

"Oh yeah, these things can fly for hours since they're so small."

"Well, let's head back up the 101, the way we came. I want to make sure I'm not just imagining it."

"Roger that."

The chopper made a wide turn and went back north. This time Nod noticed something he hadn't before. Though they were over one thousand feet above the highway, he

163

could see the bodies moving very clearly. On this pass, it looked like some of them were now turned around and walking back south. He fixed his eyes on a few Crazies as they passed overhead and, after passing, they turned and were now walking back north. A terrible thought came to Nod's mind.

"So, this route must be old hat to you, right?" he suggested.

"Yeah, we used to come up about this far when we would patrol in the Cessna," she answered. "Then we would swing out over the ocean to fly over the Channel Islands and Catalina and see how clear it was. Some of the smaller islands were clear but not really habitable. Catalina's a mess with tons of Crazies."

"Always took the same route north?" Nod inquired.

"Yeah, usually. We did a few buzzes over the Great Central Valley a few times."

Nod's thoughts darkened, but he didn't want to say much more for fear of Stephanie learning what he was thinking. He just sat there, contemplative for the rest of the trip back to Whaler's Island.

As they flew over the harbor at Avila, Stephanie slowed the chopper. "What the heck?"

"What is it?" Nod asked, snapped out of his thoughts.

"I think I saw someone on the pier," she said, swinging the chopper in a wide arc.

"Yeah, we saw lots of Crazies on the pier," Nod confirmed.

"No, I mean the university one. The research pier."

"Probably just some Crazies stuck out there."

"You ever see Crazies open a door and run inside?"

"You saw that?" Nod questioned.

"I think so. It happened really fast." Stephanie hovered a hundred yards away from the end of the pier. They saw two large buildings and a greenhouse covered in plastic sheeting in the middle.

"Looks abandoned to me," Nod decided. "Wait, why would there be a cheap plastic greenhouse at the end of a Marine Research pier? I mean, it would have cost millions of dollars to build this thing and the buildings look solid, but that greenhouse looks strictly DIY. And I see green stuff in it. Somebody is living there."

"Or they're stuck there," Stephanie posited. "The pier is blocked at the road and the town is full of Crazies. No boats in the harbor, either. If someone got stuck out there when the virus hit, there's nowhere for them to go."

"I hadn't noticed the boats, before," Nod observed. "I came here right before the virus hit and there were at least twenty boats moored all over the harbor. There was a huge fishing boat right over…there."

Nod's voice trailed off. Sticking up out of the water where he was pointing was the tall mast of a boat he hadn't noticed before. As he scanned the area, he realized there were at least a dozen smaller wrecked boats just beneath the surface nearby.

"What the hell?" Nod said, barely audible.

The sound of metal being pinged rang out followed by another. "Someone's shooting!" Nod yelled. "Head for the Protector!"

Stephanie banked before Nod even finished speaking. She flew away from the narrow concrete pier and headed towards the larger, old wooden pier. Once she dropped behind it, the other pier was completely obscured.

"Should I land on the island?" Stephanie asked.

"Yeah, go ahead," Nod answered. He pulled the portable radio out of his chest rig. "I'll radio Cal and have someone pick us up. We can assess the damage when we get there."

***

"Are you absolutely sure the shots came from the research pier?" Cal asked.

"From where we were, there wasn't anywhere else within range," Nod suggested. "We're just lucky both of those shots went through the tail section without hitting anything.

"Why would they open fire?" Tex asked.

"Well, just a few months ago we got spooked by something flying over our heads one night," Clint reminded him. "If it hovered over our group for very long, one of us might have opened fire, too."

"Should we go check it out?" Cal suggested. The harbor isn't shallow, so we'd have no problem going up there."

"Is there a bullhorn or something?" Nod inquired, using his hands to gesture that he was spit balling an idea.

"Yeah, a very loud one," Cal replied. "You want to head up there and ask them if they need help?"

"We could do that," Nod stated. "No rifles in our hands. Try to look, I don't know, maybe more non-threatening."

"Except for the twin fifties at each end," Clint pointed out.

"We'll just leave them unmanned for now," Cal noted. "Leave the rifles up here in the wheelhouse. We'll get within yelling distance, but not right up next to it."

"Yeah, let's give it a shot," Nod agreed.

"Bad choice of words, Nod," Tex laughed.

It took less than five minutes for the Protector to maneuver around the large wooden pier and come with 100 feet of the research pier.

Cal handed the microphone to Nod who looked at it questioningly. "I'm just the Skipper," Cal stated.

Nod took it and thought for a second, then put it to his mouth. When he pressed the button, a large screech sounded from above them. He winced and let go.

"Sorry, we haven't used it before," Cal apologized and turned the volume down.

"Sorry," Nod stated through the microphone. "It was still loud but not too bad. "We are a group of survivors from up north. We're currently living on the water nearby to escape the Horde of Crazies working its way up the coastline. We don't mean you any harm. We just want to know if you need any help. We could provide some supplies or a ride, maybe, if you need something. If not, we'll leave peacefully."

They all scanned the buildings, then looked at each other. After a full minute, Nod began again. "Alright, we'll be leaving then. If you have a radio, you can reach us—"

Nod's words were cut off by a door suddenly bursting open. Everyone jumped and a few reached for the rifles in the wheelhouse. A figure on crutches with his left leg dangling as he quickly moved out the door. His clothes were shabby and his hair was long and covered in a straw hat. He tried to wave his hand and use the crutches to move clumsily forward at the same time. He was yelling, but his voice wasn't

168

carrying far. A few people followed him out the door, and Nod wasn't sure if they were trying to keep him from falling or trying to stop him from coming out.

"Is everything okay?" Nod asked over the microphone.

The man was yelling at the rail and it was obvious now that they others were indeed holding him up. He continued to yell, but the nearby waves and boat engines made just below audible. Cal, sensing they were a problem, cut the engines.

Almost everyone was on the deck, trying to hear, when Tex suddenly jumped in the water. Nod started over to jump in after him, when he realized Tex was swimming fairly well. Apparently, he'd been using his time on the ocean to learn how to swim. Still, Nod began to shuck his gear to go in if needed.

A few people were getting the dinghy ready. Nod kept his eye on Tex when he finally heard what Tex had. The man clearly said the name, "Dean." Nod was now in the water quickly catching up with Tex.

Both men reached the ladder at about the same time. The shabby man shuffled toward the top of the ladder. Tex reached the top in seconds and raced to him, with Nod only a second behind. As Tex reached the shabby man, he pulled off the hat revealing long, tangled blonde hair. Tex embraced him tightly and the shabby man returned it with tears streaming down his cheek.

Nod stopped short, filled with emotion as it fully set in. The shabby man was Dean. He was alive and living with a group of hippies on a pier. He quickly joined in and made it a group hug.

***

After a few minutes of tears and strong embraces, they moved inside the building. There was a long picnic bench in the nearest building along with some makeshift bed racks. Dean explained that this group was made up of former University students and a few tourists that had been caught in Avila when the virus hit. They numbered ten in all.

When they took a seat, Nod saw Dean raise his leg with his hand to sit. There was no foot sticking out of the oversized pant leg, though.

"Your leg." Nod pointed.

"Lost it in the crash below the knee," Dean stated. "But it's been slowly growing back." He raised the pant leg to reveal what looked like a stretched out baby leg with a tiny foot. "Itches like crazy, but it's growing so I can't complain."

"And my dad?" Stephanie asked, a little hope in her voice.

"He didn't make it, Stephanie," Dean said softly. "I'm so sorry. I was with him when he went and his last thoughts were of you. He wanted me to get this to you." He pulled a necklace from under his collar. Nod recognized it as one that Conner wore.

"My mom's locket," she said through tears. She took it from him and held it close to her heart.

"Ol' Conner saved my life," Dean recalled. "Told me to jump from the chopper as we crested a rise. Instead, I fell out as the chopper rolled. Blade took my leg off clean. I saw the wreckage and crawled, rolled really, down the hill. I blacked out at some point and woke up to Conner tying his belt around my leg. He was messed up pretty bad, but he still managed to tie a good tourniquet while lying on his back. He put the locket in my hand and asked me to give it to you. Then he was gone."

"We saw him in the wreckage before we had to crash land in San Luis," Nod recounted.

"Must have taken everything he had left to save my life," Dean said with a hitch in his voice. "I passed out and woke up to these folks working on me. Billy over there." He pointed to a tall man with a 49er's ball cap on. "He was pre-Med and the closest thing they have to a doctor. He kept me alive long enough for my body to start healing itself."

"We were on the beach about a mile away," Billy stated. "We heard the bombs go off and the helicopter spin out, so we came inland to investigate. The other guy, Conner, he had a large piece of metal in his chest." He looked at Stephanie and lowered his eyes.

Nod grabbed her hand and squeezed. "It's okay," he advised. "Keep going."

"Well, it was too late for him, but we thought we could maybe save Dean, so we brought him back with us. We had to leave the body, I'm afraid." Stephanie shook her head in affirmation.

"Millie and Mom are going to be so happy to see you," Tex stated, slapping him on the arm.

"I'll be so happy to see them," Dean replied. "So, where is everyone and how did you get a big boat like that?"

Nod and Tex recounted the last few months. In all, it only took ten minutes and Dean seemed to absorb it in stride. He was happy to hear the Horde was passing and that he had a new stepdad.

"So, we should go because I really want to surprise everyone back home with you," Nod suggested. "Of course, we have room if anyone in this group wants to come along. It'll be tight but we can make do. Maybe pick up some more boats if we have to."

"I don't know," Dean shrugged. "These guys have a pretty nice set up here. Lots of fish and shellfish and vegetables in the greenhouse. I mean, it's really up to them. Wayland over there makes a heck of a kelp salad."

A young woman in the back, wearing a wide hat and baggy clothes stood up and said, "Dean, you haven't told them about the pirates."

There was a short pause, then Nod asked, "I'm sorry, pirates?"

"It sounds crazy, but yeah, there have been pirates," Dean stated with a shrug. "You probably noticed there's no boats around here, right?"

"Yeah," Nod affirmed. "Last time I was here, before the virus hit, there were dozens scattered around the area."

"Well, a lot of the people that didn't die or turn feral made for the boats to get to safety," Dean recalled, looking at the others often to make sure he was telling it correctly. "Some ended up dying or turning on the water, others just didn't know anything about boats and floated off to die at sea. A few started preying on others almost immediately, attacking other boats, mostly. They'd row up at night, climb aboard and kill the passengers or worse. They'd take anything of value."

"Same old story," Tex remarked.

"That was all before I got here," Dean said. "Fast forward to my arrival, which I don't really remember too much of, and there is basically one big luxury yacht being used by the pirates. They had killed everyone else and sunk their boats. They had left these guys alone for the most part. There was a Professor here at the time, Dr. Burnham, and she had the others remove the ladders early on. Smart lady because that was what probably had kept them safe up to then."

"That was smart," Tex agreed. "I wouldn't have thought of that."

"Dr. Burnham was brilliant," the girl with the wide hat added. "Like, useful smart, not just book smart, you know?" Nod nodded in agreement.

"Well, one night, about a month before I got here, they used ropes to climb up the side of the pier. They caught Dr. Burnham in the greenhouse and stabbed her. Took all the fresh vegetables and ran off. The doc managed to stumble away to get help but it was too late."

"Why didn't they just attack you guys outright?" Tex asked. "Pick you off as you worked." He made motion with his hands as if he was sighting through a gun.

"The pirates hadn't been on land since the virus hit," Billy added. "They didn't realize, like we did, that the virus was in the air. They didn't have any guns, just knives and bats made from old oars."

"What about you guys?" Nod inquired. "Surely you had a few rifles?"

Most of the group looked away except Billy. "It's a sore spot, I'm afraid. Some in our group didn't like guns. They were afraid of them, including Dr. Burnham. We came across numerous rifles as we scavenged, but there was always an uproar about bringing them on the pier."

Nod and Tex looked at each other in amazement. "Try not to be too hard on 'em, boys," Dean suggested. "They had lived in relative safety for over a year. But, yeah, they've since learned their lesson. Not long after they got me here, the pirates parked their boat between the pier and the land. Over the next week, they started moving closer to us. Every morning, they were a little bit closer."

"But you had guns this time, right?" Tex guessed. "Since you'd rescued my brother, you had to have been back on land."

"That day was our first trip back," Billy stated. "We had to use inflatable rafts since the pirates had sunk everything else. We hadn't been on the beach five minutes when we heard the bombs go off and raced up the mountain. Then we hurried back to the pier with Dean. No time for any scavenging. When the pirates saw we had gone back to shore, they moved their boat in the way, daring us to do it again."

"They had, however, brought something from the wreckage that proved helpful," Dean said slyly, dipping his head towards a large, black duffle bag hanging on the wall.

"The AT4's!" Nod squeaked. Dean winked at him while the others chuckled low.

"What's an 84?" Tex asked.

"An A-T-4," Nod corrected exactly as Dean had corrected him. "An RPG."

"You have RPG's?" Tex asked excitedly.

Dean pointed to a shorter guy with a green baseball cap. "Thank Lee over there. He didn't even know what they were. It was just a really heavy bag so he thought they were important to me."

"Guilty," Lee said, raising his hand slightly.

Billy continued the story. "One morning, we wake up and the pirates' yacht is no more than a hundred yards out. We can see them on the deck, smiling at us, yelling stuff about killing us and all that. Dean hobbles out the door, one of the tubes on his shoulder. He clears everyone around him and fires a round at the boat."

"You blew it up," Nod assumed.

"Nope," Dean corrected him. "I missed it by at least fifty feet." Everyone started laughing loudly and Nod and Tex joined in. "I never fired one of those things before. The round exploded when it hit the water and scared the heck out of 'em, though. They pulled out of the harbor right then and haven't been back!"

Everyone laughed out loud for several minutes. Then Nod asked, "You must have picked up some rifles since then. Someone shot at us."

The man identified earlier as Lee raised his hand. "I'm sorry, that was me. I didn't mean to actually hit the chopper, though. It was just supposed to be a warning, but I'm a terrible shot." Everyone erupted in laughter again.

# CHAPTER 13

The inhabitants of the pier decided to stay where they were for the time being. Nod left a portable radio with them so they could communicate. Most had already decided they would accompany the group when they returned to land in a few weeks.

Dean stood on the deck with Tex and Nod. The Protector was slicing through the water much faster than it had earlier. Cal was obviously eager to return Dean to his family.

"Look at me," Dean said, holding his hand up. "I'm shaking."

"We all are, buddy," Nod replied.

"What'd you tell them?" Dean asked.

"Just that we had some news about the Horde and about the pier and that I was bringing a representative back with me. The leaders will meet us at the party barge," Nod said. "Turns out Millie and Trinity are already there. A lot of the younger moms take their kids there during the day to play."

Cal slowed the boat when they were within visible distance. Because of its size, the Protector was usually anchored away from the flotilla to prevent causing a big wake. It inched along until it reached its destination. Nod, Dean and Tex used a smaller raft while the others followed in a larger one. As usual, Cal and a few others stayed aboard the Protector.

Dean kept his poncho hood up, with his long hair and beard sticking out. Nod could see his eyes filling with tears as he spotted his wife and then his mother standing on the barge. He placed his hand on Dean's shoulder and squeezed.

Sadie was standing at the ladder, ready to meet a possible new community member. Tex climbed up first and gave her a big hug. She was caught off balance by it since it wasn't that long ago she had seen him. And his huge smile didn't help.

"What?" she asked.

"Just help the old man up," Tex whispered and pointed toward the ladder. "He's missing a leg."

Sadie nodded and leaned toward the raft, which was only a few feet below the deck. She stretched her hands out and her eyes caught Dean's. It took less than two seconds for her to know exactly who she was looking at.

"Dean!" she yelled, pulling him up on the deck fast. She held both sides of his head and stared at his face. "It is you," she whimpered.

"It's me, mom," he whispered back. They embraced so hard, Dean dropped his crutch.

Hard, fast footfalls pounded across the deck and the small crowd made way. Millie stopped short of them as they parted. Sadie stepped back as Dean turned towards Millie.

"Honey, I'm home," he said softly. She leaped forward into him and grabbed tight. Nod, still on the raft, had to push up from behind so they didn't both go overboard.

Tex had already grabbed Trinity and brought her over. When Dean saw his little girl, he stretched one arm out to her and Tex handed her over.

*** 

The reunion turned into a celebration. Dean spent the evening telling and re-telling the story of his survival and pirate encounter. Of course, everyone wanted to see his healing leg. And much of what remained of the alcohol stores were consumed.

It was well after midnight before Nod and Sadie found their way home. Sadie had offered to take Trinity for the night, but Dean wouldn't have it. He wanted both his girls close for the first time in months.

"It was a good day," Sadie said with a yawn.

"Best in a long time," Nod agreed, echoing her yawn. They both stretched out in their small bed and Sadie's head came to rest on Nod's chest.

"Just having Dean back would be enough but finding out the Horde is passing soon certainly sweetened the prize. Do you really think they'll be gone in a couple of weeks?"

"Good chance," Nod replied. "We'll wait a week and go up again. I also want to buzz the ranches to get an idea how the crops fared."

"That'll be nice to know." Sadie paused. "There's something else, though, isn't there? I can tell you're hiding something. Did you meet a cute little co-ed at that pier?" She turned her head and winked at him.

"Yeah. I'm mean, yeah, there is something else. Nod stammered. "The two times I've been in a helicopter above the Horde, I've noticed they seem to react to the sound of the blades. Like they're attracted to it."

"Makes sense, them being so loud," Sadie acknowledged.

"Even when we were very high up, they seemed to react to them. If we made a course change, the Horde below shifted also."

"I don't understand, Nod. What's the problem?"

"Every week, Conner and Steph flew the same pattern across LA and up to the 101. Once they were up the highway a little, they would peel off into the ocean. I don't think they found the Horde, I think they accidently made the Horde."

"What?" Sadie asked, sitting up in bed.

"Think about it," Nod said, sitting up, too. "They flew the same pattern every week, sweeping across the city, up to the 101 for months before they noticed the Horde. And we never could figure out why they were even moving like that to begin with."

Sadie put her hand to her mouth. "Oh my god. Do you think Steph knows?"

"No, she's a terrible liar. And I don't think it adds to anything if we tell her or anyone else. It's just an idea with no proof anyway."

"It makes perfect sense, though," Sadie agreed. "Your right. We can't say anything. If she finds out, she'll be devastated. If everyone else finds out, they might string her up."

"My lips are sealed," Nod stated. "Still, if it's true, we'll have to watch how we fly. Try and make the flight paths more random. We don't want to draw any towards us when we're back on land."

They both lay back down. "Well, it's nice to know this part of the journey is almost over. I won't miss the ocean for a *long* time. Lord willing, a month from now we'll be back on dry land and things will be back to normal."

"Yep," Nod agreed. "I can't imagine any more curve balls as crazy as this."

Nod and Co. will return in

Nod 3: A New Earth